I0621554

Blaster Squad #4

Raiders of Cloud City

By

Russ Crossley

Published by 53rd Street Publishing
Offices in Gibsons, B.C. Canada and Lincoln City
Oregon, U.S.A

Blaster Squad #4

Raiders of Cloud City

Published by 53rd Street Publishing

Cover art © Can Stock Photo Inc. / isoga

Cover designed by R. Edgewood
Cover design and layout © 2016 by 53rd Street
Publishing
Print ISBN 978-1-927621-53-0

53rd Street Publishing
Head office: Gibsons B.C. Canada
www.53rdstreetpublishing.com

Blaster Squad Series

Acknowledgments

Thank you Colleen for your dedicated editing. You make me better.

Dedication

For Rita, my one true love and best friend.

Introduction

The adventures of Blaster Squad continue with somewhat of a revelation about who is behind the conspiracy to take over the galaxy. Sort of....

Thank you to the fans for their continuing support of this series, and to my team at 53rd Street Publishing for their magical work helping me to tell these stories.

See you all on our next thrilling trip to the far future. I know I can't wait.

Russ Crossley
Gibsons, B.C.
October 2016

Raiders of Cloud City

1

Keltos IV
Rigellian Star System
4123.8.9 Galactic

MARINE SERGEANT ROCKY BONES peered over the rim of the crater to see the transport machines busily moving supplies into the hold of the alien spacecraft. He dropped down below the crater wall and let his blaster rifle fall into his lap as he sat down heavily with his back to the wall. The odor of stale sweat caused by the overburdened cooling system in his blast-resistant marine battle suit engulfed him, but he ignored the familiar acrid smells of his own stink.

Beads of perspiration dotted his skin under the suit armor.

The five-kilometer run from the landing zone had been exceptionally challenging, made more so by the low gravity. Keltos IV was about the same orbital distance from its star as Mars was from Sol, and this world was also about the same mass. It was why he'd been selected to lead this new squad on this insertion. Since he'd been born on Mars, the local conditions weren't that serious an obstacle for him even with the added bulkiness of the environmental suit.

He glanced left, then right at the five members of his squad, their backs to the wall of the crater. The briefing given him by the Alliance Intelligence officer said they were battle hardened, incredibly fit troopers, but he wondered if they were experiencing some negative effects from the low gravity.

He tapped the button on the suit controls on his left arm that activated the comm unit in his helmet. "Everyone ready?" He spoke in a low voice.

A chorus of "Aye, aye, Sarge," came over the comm.

Bones allowed himself a small smile. So far, it seemed these marines were as advertised; he should never have doubted their capabilities. It still bothered him he had never seen any of these troopers before, but they were clearly enthusiastic, which he appreciated.

But he had bigger issues right now than the health of his unit. Alliance Intelligence had been right. The enemy appeared to be abandoning this outpost, as evidenced by the number of ships being loaded and readied for liftoff.

He switched comm channels. "Alpha to Mother," he said into the helmet mike.

No response.

"Alpha to Mother," he said again, as a knot of uncertainty formed in the pit of his stomach. It occurred to him that the marine starship's stealth shields may have been penetrated. The massive enemy fleet orbiting this distant world may have attacked them.

"Go, Alpha," said a feminine voice he knew was L'tal, the marine communications officer aboard the ANSS *Phantom,* the ship that had dropped him and the squad on the surface.

"Patch me through to the captain," he said, his deep voice echoing inside his helmet.

"This is Briggs," came the voice of Captain Patricia Briggs.

"Captain, it's just as we thought: the enemy is abandoning this planet. Instructions?"

"Deploy the device," she said without hesitation.

3

"Acknowledged," Bones replied before terminating the link and switching his comm to communicate with the squad.

"Mak-Tol," he called to the bulky, four-armed Lobsan to his right next to Phillips. His voice was grim.

He wondered if the squad would obey the orders as he would. They had all known when they volunteered that this was a suicide squad, so any mission could be their last. The only real questions were the unknown variables of where and when. The survival of the Alliance often dictated the where and the when they would be called on to make the ultimate sacrifice.

Destruction of this world and the supply of exotic minerals being loaded aboard the ship on the other side of this crater wall would slow down the advance of the enemy to allow time for the Alliance fleet to intercept them and stop the rebellion before it could advance any further. It was a death worth giving, as far as he was concerned.

"Yes, sir," replied Mak-Tol. He was carrying the newly developed weapon, which, when exploded, would create an artificial black hole to consume not only the planet but also any ships in low orbit. By now,

Captain Briggs and the *Phantom* would have left orbit at high speed, headed for deep space in order to be out of range when the device exploded.

Normally they would have set the device and been transported off the surface before it exploded, but they needed to be present to repel any attackers who would detect the energy field as soon as it was activated. Though the chance the rebels would be able to deactivate the device before it reached full power was minimal, Alliance Command ordered a marine suicide squad be assigned to protect the device from any interference.

"Deploy the device," Bones said. He scanned the troopers around him and saw them visibly tense; all except Mak-Tol.

Bones watched the four-limbed alien trooper unsling his pack and set it on the rock-strewn ground. He opened it and took out what would appear to the casual observer as a gleaming, stainless steel ball about the size of an ancient baseball. The difference being a triangular-shaped dark blue activation plate recessed slightly below the otherwise smooth surface.

The muscular Lobsan's gray eyes looked up from the device in one of his right hands to lock with Bones'.

Bones nodded grimly. They'd have twenty minutes after it was activated before it exploded and they accomplished their mission.

"No one move," said a high-pitched voice behind him. Bones froze. Had they been discovered? "Everyone drop their weapons, including their pistols."

Bones dropped his blaster rifle and pistol at his feet and, without having to look, he heard the clatter of rifles and pistols striking the rocky terrain.

"Stand up, Mak," said the voice Nick suddenly recognized. Mak, Bones, and the squad all stood. They were now exposed to enemy fire from the other side of the crater wall. His eyes flitted to his right and he saw several heavily armed guards were headed their way. The mission was officially blown.

Erin Hew? How could this be? Hew was a member of the squad assigned to the mission. "Hew," Bones said between gritted teeth and turned slowly to face the traitorous marine, "what the hell are you doing?"

Ignoring Bones' question, Hew continued. "Bring me the device, Mak." A burst of blaster fire created a shower of shattered rock fragments across the ground to their right. "And no tricks."

"I could just activate it," said Mak-Tol, his steady, angry gaze fixed on something to Bones' left. Hew discharged his weapon severing Mak-Tol's arm with his hand holding the device from his body. His smoking limb landed in amongst crevices in the rocky terrain. The Lobsan howled in pain.

Hew's eyes flitted to the crevice where the device disappeared then back to lock eyes with Bones. The traitor emitted a grim chuckle. "But you won't, or I'll burn the Sarge where he stands. Then I'll kill the rest of you one by one before I retrieve the device."

The muscles in Bones' arms and legs tightened as he tensed in preparation for what he was about to do. It might be suicide to try, but he had fully expected to die during this mission anyway; so what did he have to lose besides his life?

Bones heard the crunch of boots on uneven ground and picked this moment to swivel to his left and strike out with his left arm. Unfortunately, all he met was empty air. He saw the blur of a rifle barrel coming at him. Unable to halt his momentum, he stepped into the contact point with the barrel. The force of the blow shattered the faceplate of his helmet and tore into his left cheek. His face was on fire, the pain shooting across his face as the world began to disappear into a fog.

He dropped to his knees; the taste and smell of blood filled his senses.

Finally he collapsed and the squad, the planet, the universe itself seemed to disappear in a swirl of blackness. His final thought was that death had come far too easily. Not how he expected the end to come at all.

2

Unknown Starship
Orbiting Feros III
Feros System
4148.3.4 Galactic

A DEAD-EYED GAZE—irises the color of obsidian—
narrowed as they studied the screen displaying the
green and blue world hovering in the blackness
of space like a Molposan apple. Some would call
the planet beautiful. The Master called it his most
excellent future prize.

"Master," said the ship's pilot, interrupting his
thoughts.

"Are they returning?" the Master asked, his voice
a deep-throated growl. He unfolded his muscular arms
from across his wide chest, covered in blast armor
the color of his race's purplish blood, and stepped to
stand looking down at the pilot's station.

He let his arms fall to his sides, one hand stopping to grip the butt of the plasma pistol in the holster surrounding his thick hips.

It pleased him to watch the pasty-faced pilot's hands tremble and his deep swallow before he replied. The man was frightened of incurring his Master's wrath, as he well should be. "Yes, sir. Tribune Kron reports they have lifted off and will rendezvous with us within the hour."

"Good. I'll be in my quarters. Signal Kron to meet me there."

"Yes, sir."

The Master started to walk to the lift at the rear of the flight deck. He scanned the flight crew, his eyes pausing briefly on J'Pal, his mistress, a six-foot-tall auburn-skinned Estuian with a lithe, athletic body covered in a one-piece chocolate brown bodysuit. Then he shifted his attention to Rustor, his most loyal general, a four-armed Lobsan.

Rustor's slit-like eyes followed his Master, walking across the deck to the lift. Rustor's ruddy, wide face was clean-shaven like his hairless scalp, and his rugged facial features appeared to be carved in stone. His seven-foot-tall frame bulged in the formfitting microfiber jumpsuit straining to contain his muscular torso, arms, and legs.

The large blaster in its holster hanging off the left side of his narrow waist had been used to kill many of his Master's enemies and a few allies who outlived their usefulness.

A flicker of a smile crossed the Master's lips as the flight deck disappeared behind the closing lift doors. Once in his quarters, he sat in the leather executive chair behind the smoked glass desk and waved his open hand over the power sensor to activate the monitor on the desk. The screen flickered to life, displaying the symbol of a two-headed Tustin hawk holding a bloody, severed arm in its left beak. He had personally designed the symbol to inspire his forces as his empire steadily began to spread like a benevolent blanket over the whole of a galaxy that cried out for strong leadership. Soon all opposition would drown in its own blood and the new emperor would emerge from the carnage as absolute ruler bringing order to the galaxy once more.

"Display Feros III data," the Master said in a low, deep voice.

The data about the world they orbited appeared on the screen. Feros was about the size of Earth, which was the home of his most powerful enemy, the Galactic Alliance.

His hatred for the Alliance made his guts burn with fury whenever he thought of that weasel Chairman Whizzar and his smug compatriots on the Alliance Council. He detested council meetings but he had to work from the inside if his endgame were to succeed.

The atmosphere of Feros III would support many classes of lifeforms, a factor very important to his plans for this world. He needed a base of operations near the Lestrom Nebula trade route. A world in the region with a breathable atmosphere was preferable to one where his troops would need to wear pressure suits. The only world close enough to the nebula for his purposes was in the Feros system.

Two of the three large continents of Feros III were inhabited by a race of beings calling themselves Ferosians, who abhorred war and conquest even amongst themselves. Since he relished war and destruction, these peace-loving beings left him nauseated.

They will die violently, he thought grimly.

Fortunately, there was a race of aliens living on a secluded mountain plateau atop the highest mountain range on Feros III's southern continent. These aliens were the descendants of a race of explorers called the Tuple.

The original explorers had been stranded on Feros III over five centuries ago when their primitive starship crashed.

From his spies, secretly transported to the surface to gather pre-invasion intelligence, the Master learned that Ferosian legends told of a fiery ball appearing in the sky seen by millions of people that was thought to be a mythical race of gods coming down from the heavens to live high in the mountains of the unpopulated southern continent. At the time, the Ferosians had been a primitive people who believed this mythology.

A century later, a Ferosian holy man told of a domed city in the mountains where their gods now resided. Too afraid to explore the southern continent for fear the gods would become angry, the Ferosians had never explored the continent during the intervening centuries though their technological and educational levels gradually improved.

According to the Master's spies, the Ferosian myths referred to a domed city known as Cloud City, a place where the spirits of the dead reside in the afterlife for eternity.

"Such simple-headed nonsense," the Master mused under his breath. "This is going to be too easy."

Normally he would have assembled a battle fleet to sweep away the two races, leaving the planet under his control, but it was located too near the Lestrom Nebula trade route. Such a massive attack would attract the attention of the Alliance Navy. His forces weren't yet strong enough to take on the AN. More guile than he usually liked to employ was required in this instance to accomplish his goals. While he considered such soft, clandestine methods as signs of weakness in others, he knew he would need subterfuge to succeed in this case.

A signal sounded, indicating someone was in the corridor waiting to enter. "Come," he said bluntly as he eased back in the chair. He let his left hand drop underneath his desk, where he had attached a holster and a small blaster in case he needed easy access to a weapon. Too many ambitious men and women had been assassinated because they failed to take necessary precautions. He had promised himself never to let that happen to him.

The door cycled open and Tribune Kron entered and stood before him at attention. Kron gave him the straight-armed salute he had ordered all his troops to use when saluting him. "Hail, the Emperor." Kron's voice was raspy and he smelled of rainwater as if he'd been caught in a storm.

The Master gave the officer a crooked smile. "I'm not emperor yet, Kron, but I appreciate your enthusiasm."

Kron's yellow cheeks flushed darker. "Please accept my humble apology, Master. I meant no offense."

The Master eyed the officer with one eyebrow arched. "I'll let it go this time, Kron." He chuckled grimly as he released his grip on the hidden weapon and stood, letting his arms fall to his sides. "Did you make contact?" The tribune nodded curtly. "And did they agree to my proposal?" Again Kron nodded.

The Master turned away, his back now to the stoic officer. Reaching to the wide buckle on his blaster holster, hidden from Kron's view, he slowly withdrew a stiletto from a sheath secreted within the buckle. The razor sharp blade gleamed in the subdued lighting of his quarters. He let the arm holding the knife fall to his side. He grinned to himself, then turned and stepped forward while raising the knife until it was waist high. He then drove the blade under the tribune's armored chest plate, upward under his rib cage, and into the heart in a single, powerful thrust.

The tribune did not cry out but his wide eyes registered the surprise and the pain.

The officer was dead before he fell backward, the knife imbedded to the hilt in his chest, landing hard on his back on the carpeted floor with a dull thud. His lungs emptied of air in a soft sigh as his corpse sagged.

At least there would be no blood to clean up since the heart had ceased to function immediately due to the perfect placement of the killing blow. The Master was pleased with the accuracy of his strike. He straddled the dead man, one booted foot on either side of the cooling body. Reaching down, he extracted the knife and wiped the small amount of yellowish blood off the blade on the dead man's arm. He then placed the knife back in the hidden sheath.

No one would know the details of his deal with the inhabitants of the planet. He gazed at the dead tribune, the unseeing eyes still wide with shock, and chuckled grimly. *At least no one still alive.*

3

Alliance Command Station
Orbiting Earth's moon
4150.1.16 Galactic

SITTING BEHIND THE DESK in the command station's communication center, Nick Justice popped another fresh orange slice into his mouth as he struggled to listen intently to Gears over the comm explaining the upgrades to the GSS *Hunter* about to be completed at the Armstrong shipyard in Earth orbit. He bit into the fruit, causing the sweet juice to flood his taste buds. Normally it would taste sweet and acidic on his tongue and the smell of oranges would fill his senses in a pleasant way, but his brain didn't register the pleasure of this simple food. The news from his tech expert had deadened his senses.

The *Hunter* had been modified into a class of warship that made him very uncomfortable.

17

Being a mercenary often meant you had to apply force in certain situations—and have the willingness and capability to apply that force—but the introduction of plasma torpedo banks and upgraded blaster cannon batteries made the *Hunter* the most powerful Iosaijn warship ever constructed. It would be more heavily armed than most picket ships in the Alliance Navy.

Additional upgrades had also been made to the stealth shields and the protective screens, making it virtually invisible to most known sensor technology; and the new defensive screens were capable of absorbing a short-range blast from a plasma cannon.

What worried Nick most about these enhancements was it meant the Alliance might ask them to supplement the Navy's firepower during a conflict. And during any Alliance conflict that violated Nick's personal ethics, how would Chairman Whizzar and his senior admirals react to Blaster Squad refusing to act on their behalf in the event of war?

One reason Nick had left the navy was that he could no longer stomach what he saw as atrocities inflicted by the Alliance Navy against various races across the galaxy.

The most recent example was the destruction of Brimstone V by Alliance shock troops that had resulted in the loss of millions of lives almost two years ago. Such wholesale slaughter had solidified in his mind his reasons for creating Blaster Squad. The squad may be mercenaries—referred to by some as guns for hire—but Nick saw himself and his squad as champions of truth and peace. He had refused several contracts that conflicted with his personal code of ethics. Those contracts had been for large amounts of credits that would have allowed them all to retire in luxury, but Nick wasn't about to be seen as an amoral killer for hire. How would he be able to look himself in the mirror if he accepted blood money? He shuddered at the thought.

"So, Gears, when will the *Hunter* be ready?"

Gears' response was delayed as the signal travelled between Earth and its moon. When Nick's words registered, Gears responded, "I'll be leaving for Alliance Station tomorrow at 0800 hours." He winced slightly. "That is when Bones and the Kid are scheduled to return from their Earth-side *adventures*."

Nick smiled to himself. Bones and the Kid had become pals once they discovered their joint love of what they called *adult* recreation.

Gears disapproved of the friendship because he and the Kid still verbally sparred with each other. Nick decided, for the good of the team, to sit them both down at the next opportunity and talk about the issues between them and hopefully resolve this animosity they seemed to have for each other. Their personality differences, on the other hand, were another matter entirely and probably insurmountable.

At first, Nick suspected Bones' and the Kid's joint interests involved women and alcohol until he discovered they spent the majority of their recreation time attending professional sporting events and playing sports themselves against some of the best amateur athletes on the planet. Even sports they knew nothing about were a challenge to their inborn competitive natures.

They studied the sport until they felt able to compete. They particularly enjoyed learning all they could about obscure sports such as tuk-tuk polo, volcano surfing, and anti-gravity jai alai. Nick had no idea where they learned of such offbeat sports, but he was certain they had become proficient at them since they hadn't suffered any broken bones or missing limbs.

"You're sure they'll be there?" Nick asked.

"Yes, Captain. I'm sure." Gears tone suggested he had made the necessary arrangements to round up his strays before departure.

Nick long ago learned not to question his tech specialist's *arrangement*s so he just accepted Bones and the Kid would be with Gears when the *Hunte*r arrived at the Alliance command station. The trip from the Armstrong shipyard would take a couple of hours so he would plan to meet them at the docking bay at 1000 hours.

Nick wanted to get underway as soon as possible.

His ongoing disagreement with Asia Call about the Brimstone V debacle hadn't gone well, but he wasn't going to let Asia off the hook, at least not yet. Lives had been lost needlessly and he had vowed someone would pay for those deaths. His mentor claimed she didn't know who this Master was or if he or she had been involved in the events in the Brimstone system.

Nick sensed Asia was holding something back, but he knew pushing her on the subject wouldn't yield any results. She could be very stubborn.

For now, she had asked him to lead the squad on another dangerous mission on a remote planet where a larger issue was in play that required Blaster Squad's skill set.

Asia explained billions of lives were at stake as well as the future of trade throughout the galaxy. Someone had been arming one of the two races on a planet called Feros III with technology far in advance of their scientific development, for reasons as yet unknown. Asia explained she suspected the purpose was to take over Feros III after a devastating planet-wide war cleared the way for invasion in the guise of offering assistance. Billions of innocent, primitive beings would suffer and die if they failed to act.

The system was located near the Lestrom Nebula, which was a strategic key trade route in this quadrant of the Alliance controlled section of the galaxy.

The beings who live on Feros III were not spacefaring and they were technological infants by Alliance standards, so they had no idea they were about to become pawns in a greater game for control of the galaxy.

The Navy was reluctant to intervene, since Feros III was untouched by the Alliance, and had yet to undertake a first contact mission. Too much could go wrong during a first contact mission so the Navy preferred private contractors to take the risks. Then they'd step in to clean up any messes.

Nick assured Asia the differences between them regarding the last mission were on hold until he returned, given the urgency of the danger facing the civilized universe.

The possibility that the Master was behind the events on Feros III over the past few years was too tempting a personal grudge target for Nick. He had to find out for sure if the Master was involved. If he was, then Nick hoped to get closer to this mysterious figure. His guts twisted as he slept every night when he thought of the beings across the galaxy that had suffered due to the actions of this megalomaniac. He had to be stopped, even if it meant it led to the Alliance Council itself.

4

GEARS BROUGHT UP the image of the blue-green planet on the tri-screen's viewers in the middle of the flight deck, something that had been added during the last refit.

The viewers were a trio of screens set on a pedestal in the center of the deck, arranged in a triangular pattern, so every crew person could see, from their stations, whatever was projected. The old flight seats had been fixed to the deck but the new seats were designed to swivel. Being able to move his chair made Nick uncomfortable and slightly nauseous when the ship shifted position beneath him.

The old design felt solid underneath him, not like this loosey-goosey new design—as Gears referred to the changes to the *Hunter.*

Gears didn't approve of any changes to his ship unless he did them. Nick didn't entirely disagree since, as far as he was concerned, navy engineers like to change things that work perfectly just for the sake of change.

What really bugs me is they never *ask me* before *they do it*, thought Nick.

While Feros III was mostly shades of green and blue, the visible continent below them was mostly green, dotted with brown and black patches. As they orbited, a second continent appeared that was in darkness except for patches of bright light denoting inhabited areas that were large cities. From the extent of the lights, it seemed there were many, many inhabitants.

The third continent in the southern hemisphere was shrouded in clouds except for a number of black, jagged mountain peaks that stuck through the clouds like burnt candles on a birthday cake.

"Gears, where is the largest population center?" Nick asked.

The tech genius didn't respond, but the screens shifted as the magnification increased until they could see what appeared to be a large city in a valley dotted with green, red, yellow, and blue lights.

Gears began to explain just as Nick opened his mouth to ask questions. *How does he do that?* "I've been monitoring their analog radio communications and, while they are primitive by our standards, our SIN was able to translate their language after a few orbits," explained Gears. "According to the broadcasts, this city is known as Lothos and is the capital city of this continent." His eyes shifted to Nick's. He must have realized he hadn't answered Nick's first question. "Sorry, it is also the largest population center on this world."

"SIN," Nick said, speaking to the System Information Network that provided their communication links and monitored all ships systems, "What can you tell me about the recent history of this world?"

Siren caught his eye. She was seated at the engineering station as usual, with Bones at weapons and the Kid at sensors. She gave him a quizzical look. He responded with a tight-lipped smile, then shifted his gaze back to the city of Lothos on the screen. According to the declassified Intel report provided them when they accepted this mission, the Alliance had been sending surveillance drones to this world watching its development for the past three centuries.

"Please be more specific, Captain," said the SIN.

Nick thought for a few seconds, then said, "Detail changes to the planet's government over the past two years." He hadn't told his squad some background details about the mission that Asia had mentioned during their private briefing. He didn't need his team distracted by any extraneous information Asia had shared with him.

The principal concern of the Alliance was the arming of the descendants of the Tuple, who were castaway on this world centuries ago. The Tuple had constructed a domed city from the wreckage of their starship and had lived on the mountainous continent mostly undetected by the Ferosians until fairly recently.

Somehow Ferosian mythology adopted the arrival of the Tuple, whom they believed to be gods, into their culture. They called the domed city Cloud City, the place where the spirits of the Ferosian dead went to live for all eternity. Superstition had kept the Ferosians from exploring the third continent in any meaningful way for the past thousand years although they explored much of the rest of their planet.

Asia thought the only way this myth could have arisen was if someone on Feros had witnessed the crash of the starship and the building of the dome.

Most myths have a grain of truth in them, and Asia suspected whoever started the myth left the mountains and told a Ferosian about what they had seen.

SIN began to explain. "Two years ago, the Ferosians were divided into two separate governments, one on each of the two most populated continents. They appear to be on the brink of civil war."

"And why would that be?" Nick's gaze fell over his crew, who were intently watching the screens, transfixed by the SIN's tale. He smiled to himself. *We do love a good tall tale, don't we?*

"The Ferosians discovered an alien living in their midst, surgically altered to appear as one of them." The SIN paused, then added, "Before you ask, Captain, it wasn't an alien from off-world, it was one of the Tuple castaways. Details about the Tuple are meager but the Alliance Science Bureau believes they originated in another galaxy, one of three suspected extra-galactic races that migrated to the Milky Way galaxy thousands of years ago."

"How do we know any of this?" Nick asked.

The SIN didn't hesitate. "The Alliance has been sending stealth probes to Feros III for the past three hundred years.

"The last report was just over fourteen months ago."

Nick's brow wrinkled and he eyed Siren, who glared at the screen, her eyes narrower than usual. He looked back at the screen with the green and blue world passing, slowly, several kilometers beneath them. "Why hasn't any probe reported since then?"

The screens went dark, and a jumpy, digitally recorded image appeared on the screen. It was obviously taken within a planetary atmosphere, from an elevation of five thousand kilometers according to the statistics in the bottom right quadrant of the screen. The image showed a city with ordered streets, green trees and bushes lining both sides of the roads. As the probe went lower and magnification increased, Nick began to make out buildings amongst the trees and land vehicles moving on the roads. It was daytime so they could see everything relatively clearly. The planet appeared tranquil and as normal as many cities across the galaxy.

Nick expected to see street vendors selling food and drink. His mouth began to water, recalling the food vendors on Cerebral II and their delectable tuber pie with sweet jok-ol sauce. *That was good eatin'* as his great-grandmother used to say.

Suddenly on the screen, a concentrated beam of bright light broke through the trees, interrupting his concentration. The beam appeared to be headed in the direction of the probe. There was a brief flash and the screen went dark. Nick swallowed the saliva in his mouth and stared at the screen, which had shifted back to the image of the peaceful green and blue planet.

Was that an explosion? It couldn't be. The probe was in stealth mode, undetectable to such a technologically primitive species. *No way, must be something else*. Nick blinked his eyes. "SIN, what happened?"

"Analysis of the probe data suggests a plasma cannon was fired at the probe, destroying it. Alliance Intelligence lost contact with subsequent probes after they reported they were entering Feros III's atmosphere. Beyond this, AI knows nothing." The SIN concluded its report.

"You can say that again," muttered Bones.

"No, SIN, you don't need to repeat the information," Nick said quickly, shooting an amused glance at Bones. His long-time friend shrugged and crossed his muscular arms over his wide chest.

Alliance Intelligence had many faults, but their probes were incredibly resilient and almost impervious to attack. The advanced shielding and the stealth capability made them excellent spy tools that had proven useful for clandestinely gathering intelligence for the past five hundred years. Except for a direct hit by a plasma cannon, they could survive most attacks to live another day. Someone obviously knew these AI machines' capabilities and vulnerabilities.

Someone at Alliance Intelligence knew this too, but hadn't bothered to share this with Nick and the squad. Maybe this mission wasn't worth the credits they were being paid.

"Excuse me, Captain, but we're under attack," said the SIN in its usual deadpan tone.

"Defensive shields to maximum," ordered Nick. "Gears, evasive maneuvers. Get us out of here right now."

Nick dropped into the copilot's seat, his eyes flitting to the pilot's seat next to him, and saw Gears had taken over the controls manually. Most pilots had a series of pre-programmed responses to attack but Gears preferred the old-fashioned way he called flying-by-the-seat-of-your-underwear, or something like that.

31

Nick looked at the center screen of the horseshoe-shaped nest of three screens in front of him where the Kid had brought up the sensors' readings of the incoming missile. His heart raced, not from fear but due to the sudden rush of adrenaline he always experienced when the squad came under fire. These were the times when he loved being a mercenary fighting seemingly impossible odds.

Gears soon had them out of orbit and well out of range, based on the speed of the incoming projectile. It was driven by a chemical-fuelled rocket engine, not a nuclear-fuelled propulsion system as the Alliance had used for non-FTL flight for more than a thousand years. But there was something strange about the readings. They soon left the missile behind until it finally disappeared off their sensor grid.

Studying the readings of the weapon, Nick saw that, while it showed a definite radiation signature, it was unlike anything he had ever seen before. "Kid, what type of weapon am I seeing here?"

"Other than the obvious outward appearance of a chemical rocket, sir, I'm not entirely sure. SIN doesn't contain a record of this radiation type. Its power level is off any scale we're capable of measuring. Even the energy field the chairman wants us to find is not this powerful.

If the missile had struck us, we would have been instantly vaporized when the energy was released."

"Gears? Anything?"

"Well, I have a theory, Captain, if you're interested."

Nick smiled to himself. Sometimes Gears displayed uncommon uncertainty about his captain's reaction to one of his ideas, no matter how outrageous. "Go ahead, Gears."

Gears let out a slow breath, then began to explain. "The missile itself is ancient technology from our perspective, but the readings indicate it was constructed from new materials. The radiation is of an unknown type with an explosive force far beyond the Ferosians' technological level according to Alliance Intelligence reports. This suggests someone from outside their world provided them with the building materials and the radiation source for the weapon."

Siren spoke up from her seat at the communications and engineering station. Her yellow, almond-shaped eyes regarded him coolly.

"Justice," Siren said, "I think we have sufficient evidence that the Master, whoever she or he is, has interfered with this planet's technological and social development contrary to the Galactic Accords."

She had physically recovered from recent events on the mining planet Brimstone V, also known as the Planet of Doom to local miners. Nick wasn't confident that his second in command's mental state was as solid as she claimed. The disappearance of her sister, Sonara, after she left Brimstone V had been particularly troubling to Siren.

Someone had violated the accords, that much they knew for certain. Whether it was this mysterious Master or not remained up for grabs. Any violation of any of the Galactic Accords by member worlds resulted in the total destruction of the offending world and all its inhabitants. No member world would take such a chance. So it had to be someone else arming these aliens with advanced weaponry. The endgame of whoever was behind recent attacks was unknown, but Nick's hard-won experience told him something big was in the works.

Nick wasn't ready to concede her point just yet. If he did, then the Alliance Navy would take over the investigation and destroy what they would class as a contaminated world, along with all its inhabitants.

In the early days of galactic exploration and expansion, many corporations hungry for increased profits.

They had provided primitive alien beings with weapons and technology too early in their world's social and technological development, causing many primitive worlds to destroy themselves. More often, this set off deadly conflicts engulfing whole regions and hundreds of worlds across the galaxy.

After a fleet of Alliance trading ships was attacked and thousands of lives were lost, the Alliance Council acted swiftly to outlaw interference with primitive cultures citing the need to enhance trade opportunities through peaceful means.

Not that the Alliance always used peaceful solutions to rectify what they viewed as problem worlds; in fact, sometimes they caused more destruction if they considered it necessary.

But Nick wasn't about to let the Alliance eradicate another species on his watch. He'd lost far too much sleep after the destruction of Brimstone V at the end of their last mission. Nick had too much alien blood on his hands already to let this world suffer the same fate.

Something else was bothering him. "Gears, were our stealth shields operational when we entered orbit?"

Gears' ocular implant-enhanced eyes dropped to the systems screen in the pilot's station. "Yes, sir, fully functional." The slightly built half human, half Cygnus pilot looked at Nick, seated in the copilot's seat next to his. "In fact, they should never have been able to get a weapons lock on us."

"Well they did obviously, *Gearhead*," piped up the Kid from the sensor station, his tone heavy with sarcasm.

Gears' face flushed and his lips pursed but he didn't respond to the jibe by the younger human. Nick was proud of his tech specialist; Gears had finally learned to let the constant teasing by the Kid slide off his narrow shoulders. He cast the pilot a small smile. Gears nodded, though his cheeks were still flushed with color.

"Is there a way we can get close enough to use the materializer to transport to the surface without being detected?" Nick asked, changing the subject.

Gears' pale brow wrinkled. Finally, after a couple of minutes of silence during which Nick thought he could smell burnt toast, the tech specialist responded. "I've never tried it before but I could orbit their moon at high speed to create a slingshot effect.

Then we'll make a high-speed pass over Feros, activating the materializer at just the right second to place you on the surface before they have time to launch an attack."

"Great," chimed in Bones from his seat at the weapons station. "We'll end up in the middle of the ocean or merged with a mountain, or a flock of birds, or something worse. I kinda like having two arms and two legs and not drowning."

Nick looked at the former Marine Sergeant. Bones told him once about a member of a squad he was leading who turned traitor and nearly killed him. If it weren't for his unique Martian/human upbringing he probably would have died like the rest of his squad. While he could have had the jagged scar running down the left side of his face he kept it as reminder not to trust anyone. While Bones rarely talked about the incident Nick always suspected Bones tracked down the treacherous marine and took care of business as the old saying went. Nick certainly knew it took Bones quite some time to come to trust him.

Siren snorted as if she agreed with Bones. "Even if you can transport us safely to the surface, they'll shoot us on sight. We're alien invaders to these people."

Gears rolled his eyes, clearly exasperated. "Do you people think I haven't thought this through? That I'm incompetent?"

Nick scanned the faces of his chastised crew. Looks were exchanged and cheeks glowed with embarrassment. "Okay, Gears," said Siren softly. "I know I speak for us all when I say we're sorry we upset you. Of course we trust you. Please accept our apology."

"Okay," said Gears reluctantly. "Then I'll tell you about a new technology I've been working on."

"What would that be?" asked Nick, eyeing his friend suspiciously.

"After reading the Alliance Intelligence probe reports—at least the ones they allowed us access to—I noted the aliens on this planet were able to detect an intruder living in their presence." He paused. "I've come up with a solution to the problem using virtual reality technology. In my lab, I've constructed miniature VR image projection devices that encase your body like a second skin. The aliens on Feros are basically humanoid with some differences. Bipedal with one head, two legs, two arms, two eyes, and so on.

"They do have three distinct racial types and three sexes.

"One race dominates government; another the military; the third, the workforce, are the breeders for all three races. The racial features have parallels to Earth's, though some characteristics are blended differently.

"The Cretak are vaguely Nepalese with a touch of North American Caucasian, the Mallora appear primarily African mixed with eastern Martian, the Rocha are Hawaiian in appearance with some Southern Polaris Indian. Interestingly, all three races are hairless and have brilliant, jade-green irises. Other than these differences, they have two eyes, ears, legs, and arms, and are varying in height and weight like most races in the Alliance."

Nick arched one eyebrow as he eyed his friend. "So, you can make us appear to be some of them? What about their languages?" Nick knew from experience clandestine infiltration of an alien society could collapse quickly if you used the wrong syntax of the language or languages used by the alien races. It was probably why the earlier spy had been discovered. And that had led to a major disruption in this world's society. If this didn't work, the resulting fallout could be disastrous for the Ferosians, especially since they'd been provided weapons beyond their capabilities.

If they discovered another alien in their midst in spite of their changes to deal with what he assumed was an external threat, they might become suspicious of each other and start using these weapons against themselves. He'd heard of it happening before.

It was why the accords had been signed to prevent trading advanced technology with primitive species in the first place.

"They have three predominate languages," explained Gears, "with a few isolated pockets of sub-dialects in the more remote areas of the two most populated continents. I've programmed the translator implants with their principal languages. When you talk, or they do, whatever language they're speaking will sound like Galactic English and whatever you say will be in their language with perfect syntax. Some word usage will sound strange to you at first since a direct translation of the meaning will not be possible until the translator learns more of the local idioms." He offered Nick a lopsided grin. "But don't worry, it won't take long until you'll be walkin' the walk and talkin' the talk like a native."

"What's that supposed to mean?" said Siren, her brow wrinkled by her confusion.

Nick chuckled. "It means we'll be able to communicate with them."

40

Siren grunted. "Why didn't he just say so?"

Nick swallowed a laugh. "Okay, okay. Gears, what about weapons? Obviously we can't take our blasters with us." Nick's eyes flitted to Bones, whose eyes were wide in horror. He was sure the big guy slept with his blaster. Not having his weapon with him on this mission was going to be one of those pry-it-from-my-cold-dead-fingers moments.

His line in the sand. Nick didn't know what that expression meant, but if any two-meter-tall mountain of muscle wanted to draw a line anywhere, it was Bones. And no one would want to stop him if they valued their legs and arms.

Gears nodded he understood Nick's concerns with security. "You are correct, sir, our blasters would stick out like melting ice cream on a pile of steaming manure, so I reviewed the sensor scans the Kid made during our short visit to their atmosphere and discovered something interesting. They now have projectile weapons far in advance of the black powder weapons the Alliance probes initially reported." He paused as the SIN opened the access hatch to allow the holo-projector from under the command deck to move into position in the center of the nest of tri-screens.

The projector snapped on and a three-dimensional image of what Nick assumed was a projectile weapon appeared hovering above the screens.

Bones' tanned forehead creased and his dark eyes narrowed. "What the hell is that thing?"

Gears asked the SIN to rotate the image continually as he began to explain the weapon's capabilities. "The newest weapon apparently common to the indigenous people on Feros III is very similar to an ancient Earth weapon known as a semi-automatic tactical rifle. It has a steel barrel and a hard-coat black anodized finish.

"This rifle fires a 5.56 millimeter steel-jacketed bullet. Bullets are stored in a cartridge designed to be safe until the moment when you fire them. Then the bullet separates from the cartridge. When you pull the trigger of the rifle, a spring mechanism hammers a metal firing pin into the back end of the cartridge, igniting a small explosive charge in the primer within the cartridge. The primer then ignites the propellant. As the propellant chemicals burn, they generate lots of gas very quickly. The gas shoots from the back of the bullet, increasing the pressure behind it. The cartridges containing the bullets are fed one at a time into the firing mechanism from a thirty-round magazine attached to the underside of the rifle."

"It only holds thirty rounds of these *bullets*?" asked Bones with a sneer. "How do you recharge it?"

Gears looked at Bones. "It doesn't *recharge*. In ancient times, they called it reloading. As I understand it, the operator removes the magazine that contains the empty cartridges, then puts in a new magazine with fresh cartridges, then does so over and over until the job is done."

Bones scowled and crossed his massive arms over his wide chest. "How do you remove the magazine?"

Gears shrugged. "I have no idea. I'm just repeating what it says in SIN's memory core about similar historical Earth weapons."

"Does it have a non-lethal setting?" asked Siren.

Nick glanced at his second in command. *Now that's a good question*, he thought.

"No, it has only two settings: on and off," replied Gears, his voice deadly serious.

Bones snorted his frustration. "I suppose it has a firing stud so at least it won't go off until the operator intends to fire?" Gears nodded. "Good. At least that's something."

"Though the historical records state weapons of this type were frequently fired accidentally. Some historians claim as many as fifty million people were killed accidently by this type of rifle," added Gears.

Bones threw up his hands in frustration and glared at Nick. "You know I'm loyal, sir, and I'll fight anyone you ask me to, and I'll follow you anywhere. But to transport ourselves into a possible hostile situation where the locals are armed with weapons that can kill us by accident seems like too much risk, even for me."

Siren snorted derisively. "It's hard to argue with Bones' logic, but Blaster Squad has never walked away from danger and never will as long as I'm a member."

Bones turned his anger on her. "Your tenure with us can be ended quickly," he said between gritted teeth with surprising vehemence.

Siren responded with an arched eyebrow and steely gaze. Her fingers closed over the handle of the dagger she wore in a sheath on her weapons belt even when she wasn't carrying a blaster, which Nick was thankful she wasn't at the moment.

Nick raised his hands in mock surrender. "Hey, guys, let's hold on here. I realize this is a dangerous situation and extremely risky, but we have a job to do." His eyes narrowed and he let his arms drop to his sides. His gaze travelled across the faces of his crew as he added, "Billions of lives are at stake.

The Alliance could very easily destroy these people and their planet unless we discover who is behind the interference with this culture, and soon."

The tension on the flight deck ebbed as his friends appeared to relax their shoulders and the scowls and anger dissipated; even, thankfully, Bones nodded.

"Good," said Nick. "Gears, are you going to have weapons for us?"

Gears nodded. "Yes, sir. I'll provide something these people call portable guns, much like our blaster pistols that fire projectiles similar to the rifles."

"How many projectiles do the portable guns carry?" asked Bones.

Gears' pale brow wrinkled. "I'm not exactly sure. Unfortunately, the data is incomplete; but given the size of the projectiles and the size of the gun, I've designed them to carry a magazine of twelve projectiles."

Bones cursed under his breath as he turned away to face the screen on his station. "Great. We're practically naked," he grumbled.

Gears smiled. "But, good news. I determined how to change cartridges in these weapons. And you can carry five extra magazines each, stored in compartments on your holster."

Bones winced. "This thing is gonna be heavy."

Nick grinned and his eyes flitted to Siren, whose lips curled up slightly at the corners. "Okay, we should get ready for transport." He paused, uncertain how the crew would react to his next order. "I'll be leading the mission; Siren, Bones, and Gears will transport with me. The Kid will stay here to pilot the ship."

"What?" asked the Kid, a look of abject horror on his youthful features. "I'm staying here to drive? I thought Gears usually stays behind when fighting is needed."

Nick nodded. "Yes, he usually does, but I don't expect there to be much fighting on this mission." Nick eyed Bones. "There'll be no unnecessary shooting, regardless." He shifted his gaze to the tech specialist. "We will need Gears with us to decipher the Ferosian technology and determine if it has been enhanced by advanced tech."

Nick's gaze travelled until it rested on Gears. The tech specialist appeared paler than usual and his hands were trembling.

This is going to be a mission for the books, thought Nick. *I hope we make it out in one piece.*

5

IT WAS DARK when the materializer beam released them. A nearby streetlamp cast an amber glow over the alley where Nick now stood. Looking over his shoulder, he saw Siren, Gears, and Bones standing behind him. At least he hoped they were. The VR projection field surrounding them gave them the appearance of Ferosians. Their own mothers wouldn't recognize them. *This is gonna take some getting used to.*

Siren had opted for the Malloran look, while Bones and Gears appeared to be Rocha. Nick's outward appearance was Cretak. Before he'd transported to the surface, he had checked out his enhanced appearance in the mirror in his quarters.

The angular face and strong chin the VR image projection field gave him was pleasant to his eye. The green eyes that looked back at him were striking against the nut-brown complexion.

Nice cross section of racial types, *Gears*, thought Nick with a small smile playing over his lips as he scanned the faces of his enhanced squad members. He didn't want to congratulate Gears just yet. He didn't need his tech expert getting a swelled head until the mission was complete.

They were all of the same sex responsible for the workforce, hoping it would be the least conspicuous. The military and government types would, no doubt, have specific knowledge they might have trouble with. He only hoped no one asked them to breed. Things might get a little tricky if they did wish to mate. He wished they knew more about the Ferosians' mating habits and practices.

Nick made a mental note to compliment Gears about his work on the virtual reality projections. They were impressive and incredibly detailed. If he didn't know better, Nick would have thought they all looked as if they'd grown up on Feros III.

Nick was glad Gears knew how to do this because he had no clue how the tech genius made this happen. But then, software technology had never been his gift.

Before they'd transported to the surface, Gears had provided them with identity documents stating they were from the city of Blucas, two hundred kilometers north of the capital. Gears had explained that these were reasonable facsimiles but they might not be current, so try to show them as little as possible.

"Okay, let's move out. We need to find a bar or restaurant nearby where we can mingle with the locals," Nick said, his strange Ferosian voice echoing off the brick walls of the alley. Ferosians spoke in a singsong style of speech and it was another thing that would take some getting used to.

They entered a street lined on both sides with four-story red brick buildings and started toward the only dimly lighted sign that the translator device implanted in his inner ear told him indicated a bar. A swirling mist permeated the air but it didn't seem weather-related given the air temperature, and it smelled of unscented soap. *Camouflage?* Nick wondered.

There were other Ferosians of various racial types talking in small groups on the sidewalk; they walked past but took no notice of this party of aliens in their midst.

Nick froze when a four-wheeled ground vehicle turned onto the street from a side street ahead, coming toward them. It made a rumbling sound as it moved along the paved road. From the rear of the vehicle came a puff of acrid smoke, and the vehicle itself was shaped like half a teardrop with the bottom side flat where the wheels made contact with the street.

The polished metallic surface gleamed brightly in the subdued amber lights set atop poles that lined the street. The vehicle appeared to be constructed of stainless steel and seemed large enough to carry passengers as well as the operator.

This society ran on internal combustion engines using fossil fuels for energy, so the air reeked of burnt carbon. Unpleasant to the nose and the throat, and no doubt an appetite killer, another thing they would get used to the longer they spent on the planet's surface.

It came to a stop next to Nick and the others. A Ferosian wearing what was most certainly a uniform rolled down a window and called to them. "Hey, you four, who is you?"

The translator told Nick this person was a law enforcement officer. He hesitated, wondering if their cover had already been compromised. But he decided he better respond or risk starting an incident.

"Yes, officer, what can we do for you?" Nick hoped his VR image projection was smiling because that was what he was doing. *Keep it light*, he kept reminding himself.

The officer shut off the vehicle's engine and swung open the operator's door, then stepped onto the street. He wore a holster containing a gun similar to the ones they each carried and he had a rifle like the one Gears had described slung over his right shoulder by a strap. "I haven't seen you four 'fore." His eyes, the color of green grapes, scanned the four Blaster Squad mercenaries. "I knows everone arounds here."

The translator was having difficulty with the local dialect but Nick knew this would gradually improve as the AI chip learned more of the meanings and the syntax.

"I'm sure you can tell by my words, officer, we are indeed not from around here. We are workforce people from the city Blucas. We've been exploring the capital. It's our first timer here." *At least that last part is true*.

The officer's brow wrinkled as he studied Nick carefully. "You shouldn't be wandering the streets. There is a conflict on, you know."

Nick let the smile fade from his VR image's lips. "Yes, officer, we are well aware. We be over-eager is all."

The officer nodded. "Okay, citizens, be care. All hail Notkol," said the officer before entering the vehicle and rolling up the window. The engine roared to life and the vehicle started moving away, headed farther along the street until it seemed to vanish in the swirling mist.

"Notkol? Royalty of some kind?" Nick said to no one in particular. He turned to face Gears' VR image. "I don't recall you or the SIN saying these people have a Notkol, whatever or whoever that is."

Gears shrugged. "It wasn't in the data."

Bones chuckled, his singsong voice sounding strange. "Who would name their kid Prince?"

Siren grunted her acknowledgement. Nick looked at her with one eyebrow arched. She obviously agreed with Bones.

"Let's hope we find out more about the system of government around here in that bar up ahead," Nick said, nodding at the glowing yellow sign not more than a hundred meters away.

As they were watching, the entrance door of the bar slammed open, banging against the doorframe, and a Malloran Ferosian stumbled into the street where he collapsed to his knees, his dusky features swathed in blood. He cried out, then fell facedown with a wet, popping sound. He lay unmoving as Nick and his companions cautiously approached the stricken alien.

"Hey!" said a deep voice from behind them, making them freeze where they stood. "What are you doing?" said the deep voice.

Nick turned toward the voice as a very tall and very wide Rocha Ferosian stepped from the shadows of a dark alley near the entrance to the bar. His round, suntanned face was flushed and his angry green eyes glared at Nick and the other mercenaries, who had also turned to face the new arrival.

Out of the corner of his eye, Nick saw Bones' right hand had moved to his holstered weapon and his muscular frame had visibly tensed. His eyes were narrow as he saw the angry alien coming toward them.

Shifting his gaze to the alien giant, Nick saw it also carried a gun in a holster on its narrow hips and it had the rifle Gears described slung on his back, held there by a strap.

Nick detected the scent of stale alcohol emanating from the direction of the alien.

Nick decided he better head this situation off at the pass before something serious happened. "Hold, on there, friend, we're only going to the bar. We're tired and hungry." He indicted the alien lying in the street, still not moving, with a sweep of his hand. "We know not about this."

The large alien stopped and glared at Nick, his meaty hands curled into fists. "About what?" He craned his head slightly in order to see the Ferosian in the street.

Suddenly his eyes shot wide and the timber in his voice changed, becoming higher. "Jerl?" He rushed to kneel beside the bloodied alien. He shifted his gaze to glare at Nick. "Did you people do this?"

Nick grinned uneasily. "As I said, we have no knowledge how this happen. The man came out of bar and fell—"

The kneeling alien's eyes narrowed further and it's jaw tightened. "Jerl isn't man."

Oh, oh, I think I made a faux pas… Nick's great uncle used to use the term *faux pas*, and all he knew for certain was the words were French and meant something about messing up. Clearly he had messed up badly.

54

He watched the alien rise to a standing position and its long arms fall to its sides.

The alien's eyes scanned the faces of the four mercenaries until they settled on Nick. "You not Ferosian," he said in a way that suggested fact, not a guess.

The large alien spread his legs wider apart and his large right hand moved to hover over the butt of his holstered projectile weapon. "I'm count three, then we draw." His brow wrinkled deeper. "I kill you." His eyes flitted briefly to the alien still lying facedown in the street. "For Jerl."

Nick's mouth dried and his heart beat faster as a rush of adrenaline coursed through his veins. He wondered if this alien was a faster draw than he was. He hadn't tried a quick draw for a number of years. The quick draw wasn't used much anymore except in entertainment stories.

Nick shifted his feet and dropped his arms to his sides, then lifted his right hand until it hovered over the butt of his gun, mimicking the Rocha Ferosian's stance.

"One." The alien began the countdown.

It appears I'm being challenged to a duel. I'm about to find out if I'm as fast I hope I am.

6

On the street outside a bar
City of Lothos
Feros III
4150.11.4 Galactic

A SOFT MOAN came from the alien facedown in
the street as the large Rocha Ferosian counted to
two. At the sound, Nick and the alien confronting
him dropped their hands away from their guns
simultaneously.

"Shall we see if it's ok?" Nick suggested.

The large alien nodded and together they went
to stand beside the stricken being. Siren had already
knelt next to the wounded alien and rolled it gently
onto its back. Her training as an emergency medical
tech had come in handy more than Nick ever
imagined. This time her actions might have actually
prevented a shoot-out and a needless death.

Maybe even my death, Nick thought, glancing at the large alien who was leaning over its injured friend. The large alien appeared very capable with his weapon, given the wear marks on the butt of the gun in his holster.

"Jerl? It's Dok," the alien whispered softly to the injured being. From the tone of voice, Nick sensed Jerl and Dok were more than friends.

Before Nick could say anything, Siren directed a question to Dok. "Is Jerl you birther?"

Dok nodded, tears running down both cheeks; his hands were trembling. Siren scowled as she examined the injured Jerl. "The birther requires immediate medical attention. I know not your med tech," she said, her voice a harsh whisper. "Or youngling will die with birther." The words *medical tech* translated as doctor maybe? It occurred to him the translator might not be getting the language exactly right.

Dok's eyes widened in horror. He stood up abruptly and ran to the entrance of the bar and disappeared inside. "Siren, Gears, you stay here. Bones, you're with me." Nick cautioned Siren to do what she could for Jerl but not to use any off-world tech that might give them away, at least for now. She nodded her affirmation but her eyes reflected her reluctance to follow the order.

Nick entered the brightly lit bar ahead of Bones. Nick had to blink a few times to adjust to the sudden increase in light. When his vision steadied, he saw the bar was populated with fifteen to twenty Ferosians scattered among round tables ending at the wall farthest from the door, where a long wood and steel bar ran the length of the room.

Behind the bar was a Ferosian who glared at the new arrivals; his head was round as a billiard ball and white as snow. He had a ring of mouse-brown hair around his otherwise bald head.

Ignoring the bartender's out-of-place appearance and the stares of the patrons, Nick walked across the room to approach the bar. The bartender watched him, his eyes flitting to either side of the room as if he were looking for backup.

Nick slapped the smooth surface of the bar top when he arrived. "I look for Dok," he said, trying to inject some fierceness into the singsong lilt of his VR projection's voice synthesizer.

The bartender tilted his head to the right side of the bar. Nick looked in the corner and saw a man-sized box with a folding glass and wood door containing Dok. He appeared to be talking to someone, speaking into a device unlike anything Nick had ever seen.

Dok placed the device in a holder, then swung the door of the box open on squealing hinges and stepped into the barroom. The fear on his face made Nick feel for the poor being.

"Is help on way?" Nick asked the distressed Dok as Dok approached the two mercenaries.

"Yes, but I don't have funds to pay…" His voice trailed off to a whisper.

The pain in his eyes and tone made Nick's blood seem to freeze. He had never experienced such heartfelt anguish. Luckily, contrary to his orders, Siren took this moment to appear in the entrance doorway leaving it open to the street beyond.

Nick looked at Bones, who scowled back at him. Bones was right—it was ridiculous to charge money for medical treatment. *What kind of barbarian runs this world?*

Nick looked at Siren's VR projected image. Her projection's high, light cocoa-colored cheekbones were flushed a reddish hue and her emerald eyes blazed with anger. "Is there anything you can do, Siren?"

Siren had transported to the surface with medical supplies and tools in a pack she had on her back.

The pack would appear to the casual observer on this world as normal household items like a portable radio—though Gears had attempted to explain what a radio was, Nick was still confused about its purpose—salt shakers, and eating utensils. Gears had modified these items to transform into medical scanners, a drug delivery device, and a field-dressing dispenser in case any of the squad required urgent medical care during this mission.

The problem was, if they helped these aliens, it might add to Dok's suspicion that they weren't Ferosian. But Nick couldn't stand by and do nothing when Siren might be able to save a life. Nick and Bones went outside onto the street once again to see if they could help Siren treat the injured alien.

Nick moved closer to Dok and placed one hand gently on his shoulder. "Dok, we might be able to help."

Dok's watery eyes lifted and looked into Nick's VR projected ones. "How?"

Nick steeled himself, then explained they had acquired some new technology before they left Blucas. "To treat the injured during the conflict," Nick finished, hoping this weak cover story sounded credible enough until they were able to slip away. If Dok didn't believe him, he had no backup plan.

"Anything," Dok said, his broad shoulders slumped. "Jerl is my only chance."

Nick noticed Dok's words were clear, indicating the AI chip was becoming adjusted to the local inflections in the language. "What do you mean by only chance?" Nick asked as Siren started to scan Jerl.

Dok grunted in a very human way. "My mate was killed in a recent attack. All that remains is Jerl and the youngling." The alien sighed heavily. "My family line ends with us."

The way Dok spoke of family gave Nick the impression that family bloodline was very important in this society. Nick assumed these aliens mated for life, hence Dok's belief that Jerl was his only chance made perfect sense.

"What do you do?" Nick asked, trying to distract Dok from what Siren was doing by engaging him in small talk.

Dok peered at Nick, his eyes curious. "You really aren't Ferosian, are you?"

Oops. Now I've done it. There was obviously no point in hiding it anymore. "No. I'm sorry, but we're not enemies if that's what worries you." A soft moan interrupted them and Jerl sat up, supported by Siren's arm around the back.

Dok's eyes brimmed with tears and he crouched next to Jerl and grasped one of Jerl's hands. "Jerl, my love. How do you feel?"

Jerl gasped for air, then in a soft whisper said, "I've felt better."

Dok's eyes shifted to Siren, still supporting Jerl. "Is the youngling okay?"

Siren nodded, her lips pursed into a thin line.

The sound of a whistle grew louder with each passing second, cutting through the swirling mist to echo off the brick buildings. A ground vehicle appeared, a device on the roof over the driver's compartment making the whistling sound, which was very loud now. Other than soft amber headlights, the vehicle displayed no lights or symbols to indicate it was a medical vehicle.

It came to a stop and the driver, a Cretak, stepped out first. A tall, muscular Malloran joined the driver, coming from the passenger side of the vehicle. "Emergency?" asked the driver.

Dok stood and walked toward the driver, his faced a blank mask free of emotion. He stopped, his arms hanging limp at his sides. "I am Dok. Jerl, my birther, has been injured. Jerl carries my deceased mate's youngling."

Nick eyed the scene before him, wondering what was happening. The two new arrivals exchanged glances. Then, as if time had slowed, the Malloran pulled a gun from the holster on its hip and shot Dok twice in the center of the chest, accompanied by startlingly loud bangs and a cloud of blue smoke. Two round spots of red blood had appeared on Dok's chest where the bullets entered his body, growing larger with each passing second. The air was suddenly permeated by the odor of coppery blood mingled with the acrid smell of burnt gunpowder.

Dok didn't make as sound as he fell backward, landing with a hard, wet, smacking sound on the pavement. His eyes were wide but unseeing. He was clearly dead.

Bones and Gears and Siren had their own guns out, pointed at the two aliens. Nick swallowed hard, his heart pounding in his chest. He suspected this would end badly.

7

On the street outside a bar
City of Lothos
Feros III
4150.11.4 Galactic

"DROP YOUR WEAPONS," Bones said between gritted teeth. Again the two aliens shared a look, and for a second Nick thought they might fire on him or the others.

To move things forward, Nick pulled his gun from the holster and joined his friends by pointing it at the two aliens. "We have you outnumbered," he said, watching the two sets of alien eyes for signs they might try to fight their way out.

They once more exchanged glances, then lowered their weapons to their sides. Feeling relieved, Nick told Gears to retrieve their guns, which he did. "Sit down on the sidewalk," indicted Nick with the barrel of his gun. The two aliens complied.

"Now tell me why you shot Dok."

The two aliens visibly hesitated and glanced at each other again, their confusion evident on their faces.

"What is it with you people?" Nick said angrily, immediately regretting his words when he saw their faces sag and the questioning look in their eyes.

Nick took in a deep breath, then let it out slowly to calm himself. Finally he said, "I'm sorry, but you just killed Dok; and while I didn't know him well, in fact we had just met, his birther is injured and we offered to help. Now Dok's dead."

The Malloran spoke first. "Dok wanted us to kill. The youngling will carry the bloodline. Dok became redundant." The alien's eyes narrowed. "You aren't Ferosian or you would know this is our way when one of a trio dies."

Nick wanted to scream in frustration but he swallowed his anger instead. The Alliance data about this world was badly lacking because Alliance Intelligence clearly didn't understand this culture. Whoever had sent the surgically altered spy to infiltrate this culture had done them a terrible disservice. Now they were suspicious of anyone out of the ordinary, even those who meant to help them like Blaster Squad.

This made Nick's job doubly difficult. Now he needed to assess the damage to this world not only due to the introduction of advanced weapons, but due to the social contamination they suffered. From what Nick had read, very few worlds survived such contamination.

"Never mind about me. Jerl needs help."

The large Malloran didn't respond for several seconds, his eyes seemingly searching Nick's face for signs of his origins. Finally the being's eyes relaxed and his shoulders eased. "My name is Oklo," said the large alien. Oklo indicated the being to the right with a tilt of his head. "This is Pucrat. We are emergency medical doctors. If you let us, we will help Jerl and take the birther to the hospital for treatment."

"You mean the same *treatment* you gave to Dok?" Bones growled bitterly.

Nick glared at the big man, knowing he would shoot these two aliens down in cold blood unless Nick managed to stop him.

Oklo didn't seem bothered by Bones' overt aggression; the alien appeared calmer than Nick would be under similar circumstances. "No, of course not."

Suddenly two law enforcement vehicles appeared from the mist that seemed to have gown thicker in the last several minutes, as had a wet, musty scent that wasn't unpleasant but left a film in the mouth and on the tongue. One vehicle appeared from the left, the other from the right as if they were boxing them in.

Nick sighed inwardly; he knew Bones would react badly to being trapped. He looked at Siren and saw she had taken a fighting stance, her gun barrel directed at the vehicle to their left.

A voice came from a speaker affixed to the roof of one of the vehicles. "Drop your weapons or we will fire. You have ten seconds to comply."

Nick lowered his gun. "All of you drop your weapons. Right now!" Nick snapped the last words at Bones. He then let his gun slip from his fingers until it dropped to the street with a clatter and skidded away across the pavement.

"Step back. And raise your arms," ordered a tall, gaunt Malloran, who stepped out of one of the vehicles to confront them.

Nick and the others, including the two medical techs, stepped away from the weapons on the pavement. Siren's eyes flitted back and forth across the face of the officer. Nick knew she was looking for an opening to attack him.

She was a master at several martial arts and could incapacitate or kill any opponent with her arms and legs within seconds. All she needed was they be momentarily distracted. But this officer kept his eyes fixed on them and his gun at the ready as, no doubt, did another officer in the second vehicle. *I think they used to call this itchy trigger fingers or a Spanish standoff?*

The second officer, also a Malloran, appeared from the second vehicle with his weapon drawn and began issuing orders, careful to remain out of range of Siren. "Get their guns." The first officer holstered his weapon, then quickly picked up the squad's discarded guns. He then placed the guns in a compartment at the rear of one of the law enforcement vehicles.

"You two," said the second officer, indicating the two emergency doctors. "Take your patient to the hospital."

The two doctors nodded and soon had Jerl loaded onto a portable bed and placed in the rear of the emergency vehicle.

The vehicle's engine rumbled to life and the whistle began to sound again. It sped off and quickly disappeared in the swirling mist. The whistling sound became warped and eerie until finally it too was swallowed by the mist.

"What are you going to do with us?" asked Nick.

The second officer moved from the rear of the vehicle where his partner had stored the guns. In his right hand he held a gun that made Nick freeze. He was holding a blaster and he had leveled it at Nick.

"Nick!" It was Gears. "That's a—" Before he could finish, the officer directed the blaster at the tech genius and fired. Gears dropped to his knees, then sagged to the street, his disguised body limp as if his skeleton had disappeared. The VR field surrounding Gears blinked, then went off, revealing his true appearance.

Before Nick could voice a protest about him shooting Gears, the alien turned the blaster toward Nick and fired. He too was enveloped in a field of blaster energy and the world around him disappeared as his vision clouded, then the darkness engulfed him.

8

NICK BLINKED until his vision cleared. His nose and mouth were dry but the smell of toast and coffee invaded his senses. He found himself looking into the compassionate, yellow, almond-shaped eyes of Siren without her VR image projection field.

"Siren?" Nick said, his voice raspy. After clearing his throat, he asked, "Where are we?"

Nick moved his hands and realized he was lying on a bed. A soft bed. He was wearing a one-piece gray jumpsuit of some kind, but his face, hands, and feet were bare.

He lifted his head enough to look at his surroundings. A black wood-burning stove sat in one corner of the room, the red and yellow flames visible through the barred grate on the front. He detected a slight smell of wood smoke in the musty air.

There was a large, wood-framed window to his left and he could see what appeared to be snowflakes drifting down against a backdrop of a murky, slate-gray sky. A wood door was across the room next to a rough looking kitchen with a wood counter. Unpainted shelves ran part way up the wall near a sink with some sort of hand pump. An oblong-shaped box sat in one corner of the kitchen. He assumed this was something designed to keep food from spoiling.

"We're in a cabin provided by the Tuple rescue team. Gears and Bones went off to meet with them to discuss a few things." Siren averted her eyes and Nick knew immediately she was hiding something from him. Ever since he had known her, she had never lied to him but she was skilled at not telling him things that were *edgy,* as she put it.

"Okay, Siren, tell me what you're not telling me," Nick said, feeling immediately more alert. Engaging a problem head-on helped him focus his mind to clear out the cobwebs of sleep and disorientation.

After several seconds of silence, her eyes landed on his. Her lips had formed a serious line and the tension on her face was evident. "We're not supposed to be here," she began. She paused, then added, "The Tuple have been trying to stop the Ferosians from getting advanced weapons."

71

"Before we go any further, can I eat first?" Nick said when his stomach growled. It was as if the smell of the coffee and the toast were calling to him.

Siren rolled her eyes and sighed. She patted his leg. "Sorry, Nick. I've been practicing this speech but I forgot about your needs."

Nick smiled weakly. "No worries, my old friend. I'm fine." *Now who's lying*? He sat up, his arms extended, his hands pressing on the mattress on either side of him. The room was spinning and his flesh felt clammy as perspiration beaded on his forehead, then quickly the moisture covered his arms, legs, and the rest of his body in slick damp.

Siren laid an arm across his shoulders, wrapping her hand around Nick's arm to steady him. "Nick, please stay here. I'll bring you a cup of coffee and some toast."

She released him as Nick closed his eyes and sucked in a couple of deep breaths. He had been shot with a blaster before but had never experienced such strong residual effects. He sensed Siren returning.

He opened his eyes in time to watch her sit down beside him on the bed. Thankfully his vision had cleared. He puffed out his cheeks and blinked furiously, hoping to clear his still foggy brain too.

"What did they do to me?" he asked as Siren handed him a black porcelain cup. Nick wrapped his hands around the warm cup. The smell of freshly brewed coffee wafted over him, enveloping his senses in the comforting nutty aroma.

"They didn't do anything to you. After the blaster," she added. "You're suffering from altitude sickness," Siren explained.

Nick took a sip of the coffee and relished it as the earthy liquid washed over his tongue, then down his throat as he swallowed. "Okay," he said, elongating the word. "So back to my first question, where are we?" He reached for the piece of toast Siren had in her left hand and, after grabbing it, stuffed one corner into his mouth. He took a bite, chewing the dry bread, his eyes looking expectantly at his second in command.

"Nick, we're on top of the highest peak on the third continent. The peak is under a pressure dome but we're still affected by the altitude. The mountain is higher than Olympus Mons on Mars."

Nick shifted his gaze to the window, where he saw snow still falling in large flakes but no trees or any signs of a pressure dome like the ones he'd seen on Mars and other Alliance worlds.

"Sorry, Siren, but this doesn't make sense. It's snowing outside and I don't see a dome."

She nodded. "I know. It takes some getting used to, but the Tuple have technology far beyond anything we've seen anywhere else in the Alliance."

It occurred to Nick he might still be asleep. *This has to be a dream.* "Pinch my arm," he said. Siren shrugged and did as he asked. Nick winced. *Damn, she pinches hard.*

"Okay, so this is real. I know you said they're meeting with the Tuple rescue team but I want to know exactly what they're *discussing* and why."

Siren cleared her throat as she shifted her bottom until she was sitting closer to Nick. Speaking softly she said, "Gears and Bones are hoping to learn the source of the weapons and technology the Tuple seem to possess. If Alliance Intelligence is correct and the Tuple are stranded travellers from another galaxy who have been here for centuries, then why are they only revealing this advanced technology now?"

Nick nodded, understanding they were probably being monitored. Siren was correct to be cautious. Something larger was going on here, far beyond their mission of monitoring and surveillance. The Alliance had set them up at a critical juncture.

It had to be something big was about to happen and they would have to act or the Ferosians and the Tuple would be wiped out. Someone wanted this planet for its strategic value. And Nick had an idea who that someone was.

"Have you, Gears, or Bones detected any signs that point to the Master's involvement?"

She nodded and her eyes narrowed.

Nick grunted. She couldn't reveal any more details, at least not verbally. And not in this cabin. Looking around, he spotted a trap door in the floor in the center of the room.

"How about we go there?" He indicated the trap door with a slight nod of his head.

"You strong enough?" she whispered. He offered her a small shrug and a weak smile. Siren stood and moved to the trap door. There was a round steel ring set in a hole in the wood. She grasped the ring in one hand and pulled it up toward her. The door creaked opened until it stopped with a thump, resting against its steel hinges. Thankfully there was no dust or unpleasant odor coming through the open door.

Siren exchanged a questioning look with Nick, then she peered into the door.

"It's dark," she said. Looking around, she scanned the cabin. "I think there's a portable lamp here somewhere." Her eyes widened when they settled on a long black tube shape on the counter next to the sink. She walked across the cabin to retrieve it, then walked back, looking the tube over to find the on switch. Nick wondered why, if these Tuple had such advanced tech, they had switches and wooden trap doors with steel rings for handles.

Then they had blasters and the technological knowledge to construct a dome at the top of a mountain several kilometers above the surface of this planet. And somehow the Tuple transported Nick and his team here from a continent half a world away. It was an odd mix of old and new tech and it bothered Nick; he might be missing something important in all this.

Siren snapped on the portable lamp and a beam of white light sprang from one end. After kneeling on one knee, she focused the beam of bright light into the opening, panning the beam around the space beyond the door. "There's a ladder leading to a room that appears to be designed for storage. There are wooden barrels and bulky-looking sacks piled on top of each other in several stacks around the room," she said. "You still want to check it out?"

Nick nodded, then gritted his teeth and managed to struggle up until he stood on trembling legs. Siren moved to support him but he waved her off. "No," he said, "I am going down that ladder. Are you coming with me?"

Not waiting for an answer, Nick sucked in a deep breath and straightened his shoulders, then took two steps forward until he stood gazing into the darkness beyond the opening in the floor. *I will make it*, he told himself, pushing aside a brief wave of dizziness.

Swallowing hard, he shivered. His skin and clothes were soaked with perspiration as if he had a high fever. But he was determined to push aside his personal well-being so he and Siren could talk in relative privacy. He needed to know what was happening so they could get out of here alive. He had a sense of dread bubbling up in his guts that he couldn't shake.

He stepped slowly onto the top step of the ladder. "Shine the light here," he said to Siren, whose eyes brimmed with concern for him. She shifted the beam of light onto the steps, chasing away the darkness. He moved down one step at a time until he was at the bottom looking up. "Siren?"

The darkness enveloped him briefly as she made her way down the ladder after him.

Then she swung the light around the room to confirm they were alone. It was a storage room with wooden barrels and the stacks of bulky sacks, just as she'd described.

She swung the beam around them after she reached the bottom rung of the ladder. Then she focused the beam on the ceiling overhead so the light defused around them and they could see each other clearly.

"What have Bones and Gears learned so far?" Nick whispered.

Siren's eyes narrowed and her lips formed a thin line. "Not much. The Tuple have an arsenal of blasters, both pistols and rifles, but they don't have chemical rockets as far as we know, and we have yet to find any signs of the energy used in the warhead."

Nick regarded Siren carefully. "You said the Tuple were a rescue team. Why did we need rescuing and from whom? And why did they stun us?"

Siren's expression brightened. "Oh, they didn't stun *us*, sir. They stunned you and Gears."

"Only us?" *Just my luck. Sometimes it's not so good to be the boss.*

Siren nodded. "Yes, sir. They then transported us here." She shook her head. "Somehow they knew you were the captain."

Nick decided to change the subject. He wasn't going to take this personally. Captain goes down with the ship. Nick had never known exactly what this expression meant since in space as there is no up or down, but he was the captain so it was safe to assume incapacitating the commanding officer made him a target. Of course how they knew who he was added more complexity to this mystery. "You said they have advanced technology beyond anything in the Alliance. What kind?"

A frown creased Siren's brow. "Well, sir, they transported us by opening a doorway that appeared out of thin air. We simply stepped through. We were there and now we're here. It wasn't a materializer, at least as we understand it." She paused and her cheeks flushed. "Gears said he had no idea how this technology works."

Nick looked at her quizzically. "As if it were magic?"

Her eyes widened. "Yes, sir."

Nick considered her words for several seconds before speaking. "You know this means they could transport aboard our ship at any time?" She nodded. "So why were we attacked by a chemical rocket?"

"I may have the answers you seek," said a deep voice speaking perfect Galactic English from somewhere in the shadows to their right.

Nick's right hand moved instinctively to where he usually wore his gun, but he froze when he heard the unmistakable sound of a blaster being drawn from a holster.

9

Tuple Pressure Dome
Cloud City
Feros III
Galactic date unknown

"WHO ARE YOU?" said Nick, trying to convey force into his voice though the dizziness was again creeping into his consciousness. Siren moved to stand beside him and wrapped her strong right hand around his arm to steady him. His eyes flitted briefly to hers and he caught the look of concern in her eyes. The shake of his head was almost imperceptible except to someone like Siren, who knew him so well.

A figure stepped out of the shadows and Nick's heart skipped a beat. The being before him was saurian in appearance. It had narrow, bright green eyes and a wide mouth filled with razor sharp teeth. The skin was a mottled battleship gray and forest green.

It was a biped with two arms and legs, and the oval-shaped head was devoid of hair. In one large hand, complete with talons, it held a standard issue Alliance blaster, which was aimed at him. It wore a black leather sleeveless vest and pants, and thick-soled boots were on its feet. Its arms were thick and muscular.

"My name is Tealmyn. I am the security chief."

Nick let a slow grin play across his lips. "If you're the security chief, why are you threatening unarmed people with that blaster?"

The alien officer's almond-shaped eyes shifted to the weapon in its claw-tipped fingers, then back to Nick.

Nick wondered if this officer would shoot first and ask questions later. He'd had no experience reading a saurian for signs they were considering his question or were about to kill him. *I guess I'll know one way or the other in the next few seconds.*

Tealmyn slowly lowered the blaster, then slipped it into the holster on the belt surrounding its thick waist. "My apologies, Captain. I thought you might be armed."

"How, when your rescue officers took our weapons?"

Russ Crossley

The Tuple security chief seemed to cringe in a surprisingly human manner. "Recently we learned your people are very...uh...resourceful."

Nick smiled to himself, then his stomach twisted after Tealmyn took a step closer; the scent of raw fish filled his mouth and nose. Nick swallowed and said, "I gather you've met Bones and Gears?"

The alien's eyes peered curiously at him. "They said their names were Musty and Rocky?"

Behind Nick, Siren snorted derisively. Nick glanced over his shoulder at his second in command and gave her a disparaging look. She mouthed a silent apology.

Nick looked back at the alien to see Tealmyn's puzzled expression. "Sorry. You were saying something about Gears and Bones?"

"Yes," said Tealmyn, ignoring Nick's reference to his squad members by their nicknames. "They tried to blow a hole in the dome wall."

Oh, no. Nick felt his face grow cool as the blood drained from his cheeks. *They didn't...of course they did.* "I'm so sorry. I hope no one was hurt." Nick wondered if Gears and Bones were still alive.

Tealmyn's eyes narrowed and his mottled brow wrinkled.

"No. We managed to stop them before anyone was hurt. We have them in confinement."

"I'm puzzled because, if we were attacked, we might not react with such...congeniality."

Tealmyn looked at Nick, his expression and eyes unreadable, without saying anything for several seconds.

The silence is deafening, thought Nick, knowing how ridiculous this ancient expression sounded, but the silence was unnerving him. He wondered if he had insulted the alien officer. He was about to ask when finally Tealmyn spoke.

"We don't kill intelligent beings. We are dedicated to peace through communication."

"But you attacked our ship in orbit with a chemical rocket carrying a radiation weapon," interjected Siren.

Just what I was going to ask.

"No, that was the Ferosians," explained Tealmyn.

Nick's heart skipped a beat. "How can that be? They don't have the technology to launch such a weapon."

Tealmyn eyed Nick. "You need to see something. Something important."

Nick swallowed hard and the earthy walls seemed to be closing in on him. He had a bad feeling deep in his gut that what he was about to learn wasn't good. And probably not good for anyone in the galaxy.

10

Tuple Pressure Dome
Cloud City
Feros III
4150.11.5 Galactic

"Justice to *Hunter*," Nick said over the portable comm supplied by Tealmyn. He was seated behind the desk of the security chief, looking at the haggard features of his squad seated on the long sofa across the room from the glass-topped desk. Deception was over; it was time to build trust.

A curved wall of shaded glass ran over their heads from the floor to disappear in the curve of the wall through which was visible the expansive snow-covered landscape, dotted with ragged spikes of black lava rock poking randomly through the white drifts. The slate gray sky boiled with windswept clouds. No doubt, if they left the protection of the Tuple dome, they would either freeze to death or die from lack of breathable atmosphere.

According to Tealmyn, the air at this altitude was as thin as the air on Mars in Earth's system, which had been undergoing radical terraforming over the past five centuries; but so far, Mars still had a barely breathable atmosphere.

Any way you slice it, we'd be dead in seconds out there, thought Nick after the Tuple security chief explained the local conditions. It amazed him the Tuple had managed to survive the crash on this mountain centuries ago, never mind how they had survived the local weather.

Of course, the air in here wasn't exactly Earth normal. As you'd expect for a saurian race, the atmosphere within the dome was thick with humidity—truly laden with moisture—and smelled of swamp. It took getting used to to feel comfortable in this environment, but the worst part was never feeling dry even after having a cool shower.

Nick fared the best in these conditions due to vacations he'd spent with his great-grandmother on Cestus IV, a swamp-covered world where his great-granny Ophelia hunted alligator-like creatures for food and their hides. The hides were highly prized throughout the galaxy, being used to manufacture shoes, coats, and tabletops.

He didn't really enjoy hunting, but it was the way his great-grandparents' families had made their living for centuries, so who was he to question their practices.

"Captain!" an excited Kid's voice erupted over the alien comm. "Are you okay, and the others—"

"Take it easy, Kid, we're all okay. A little battered and bruised but we're fine." His eyes drifted to Bones, whose right cheek was swollen, marred by a large purple bruise. Gears, seated beside him, had a gash across his forehead, which had been oozing blood until Siren used her portable wound sealer to close the tear in his flesh. The Tuple had been aggressive but hadn't intended to kill when they stopped these two from blowing a hole in the dome wall.

Gears and Bones told Nick they had planned to escape through the tear in the dome. Gears explained he and Bones had stolen Tuple environmental suits for use when they went outside the dome. Though they were designed for Tuple physiology, Gears had adapted them for human use. If anyone could adapt an alien environmental suit, it was Gears, so Nick didn't doubt him.

But after Tealmyn showed him the blueprints for the massive plasma gun being built by the Ferosians, he knew they needed to befriend these aliens if they were going to discover whoever was behind supplying the Ferosians with these advanced weapons.

Tealmyn claimed they had no knowledge of who supplied these weapons or how they were delivered. He did tell Nick they had raided several Ferosian supply warehouses. This was how they had managed to have blaster pistols and rifles. Nick was glad they did because, if they'd used the projectile weapon to subdue him, he would very probably be dead right now. There was something to be said for non-lethal weapons.

"What are your orders, sir?" asked the Kid.

Nick smiled to himself. The younger man was often high-strung and wore his emotions on his sleeve but he knew enough to follow orders.

"When I send the signal, probably in the next fifteen minutes, I want you to transport us to the ship. We'll be bringing a Tuple security officer with us." His eyes shifted to Tealmyn, whose saurian features and inky black eyes remained passive. "I'll have further instructions after we're aboard. Understood?"

"Completely, sir. I have a fix on your transmission. I'll be in position in ten minutes."

Nick closed the comm link and eased back in the chair, emitting a deep sigh from between pursed lips.

"What's wrong?" asked Siren, who stood and walked to the window, her combat boots making a gentle thump with each step until she overlooked the expansive landscape. The area was partially in shadow. It would be night soon. She crossed her arms over her chest, keeping her attention on the lifeless mountain-scape retreating into the distance where it disappeared in a cloudbank.

Nick glanced up at his second in command, wondering why she hadn't protested his decision to interfere in the local situation, which could be interpreted as a violation of the Galactic Accords. "I'm worried," he said, failing to keep the tension from his tone.

"About what?" asked Gears, who had joined Siren, standing next to her staring out the glass of the dome wall. "The Accords, perhaps?"

Nick shook his head. "No. I'm wondering if we're doing the right thing by taking out the Ferosian weapon."

"Are you having second thoughts?" asked Tealmyn.

Nick detected no sense of threat or even mild concern in the alien's voice. But he hadn't known this race for very long, so he would ask Gears and Bones in private later their opinion of their host.

Nick shrugged and offered the alien security chief a tight smile. "No, just keeping my options open is all."

"We must destroy the weapon before the Ferosians use it on each other in their current conflict," said Tealmyn. The muscular saurian alien's eyes narrowed. "The ramifications for the planet will be catastrophic if we delay any further."

Nick nodded as he stood from behind the desk and walked to the center of the office. "I agree, Tealmyn, but do you think bombarding the Ferosian with plasma torpedoes and raking their facilities with blaster cannon fire from orbit is the best way to destroy their capabilities?" He knew an attack would kill a lot of Ferosians as well as destroy their heavy weapons. And it would erase any chance they had to discover who supplied these weapons.

A much better plan, in Nick's view, would be to infiltrate the warehouses and see the weapons for themselves, only Tealmyn said the warehouses were booby-trapped to self-destruct if anyone other than a Ferosian attempted to enter.

Sure, the alien weapons would be destroyed, but they'd be killed along with a lot of the locals. Nick didn't think this was a balanced approach to the problem, which was why he'd agreed to Tealmyn's plan. Only now, he *was* having second thoughts.

Nick now stood in the center of the office where Bones, Gears, and Siren joined him. Tealmyn's eyes followed them. "We'll see you on our ship as soon as you don your environmental suit." He paused and locked eyes with the alien security chief. "When can you be ready for transport?"

"Fifteen minutes, Captain Justice," replied the alien.

"Good." Nick raised the portable comm unit. "Kid, four ready for transport."

Nick felt the welcome tingle of the materializer beam on his exposed flesh, then the office around him began to fade. A moment later he found himself standing on the materializer platform in the familiar and comforting surroundings of the *Hunter's* transportation bay, looking at a grinning, rosy-cheeked Kid. *Well, doesn't he look none the worse for wear,* thought Nick. He winced as he took a step to the edge of the platform and felt a thigh muscle twinge in his left leg. *Unlike us.*

"I never thought I'd say this, Kid," said Bones sarcastically, stepping off the platform with a grunt, "but I'm happy to see your ugly mug."

Nick stepped off the platform, as did Gears and Siren, who joined him at the control station for the materializer. "Okay, we'll have a group hug later; right now we have fifteen minutes until Tealmyn signals he's ready for transport, and I need to tell you all something before he gets here."

Siren grumbled. "He's using us, of course."

Nick nodded. "Yes, but the reasons he wants us to attack the Ferosians is far more sinister and complicated than it first appears." Siren arched an eyebrow. Nick continued. "I suspect Tealmyn is not a Tuple."

Gears' pale face registered his surprise. "Then who is he?"

"How many Tuple have you actually seen?" Nick directed his question at Gears, Siren, and Bones.

Bones spoke for the group. "I'd say around a dozen or so." Gears shrugged and Siren scowled.

Nick turned his head slightly toward Gears. "Doesn't the Systems Information Network need a full diagnostic test?"

Gears appeared confused for a brief second, then Nick's true meaning appeared to register on his features. "Yes, sir. But as you know, the SIN will be offline for six hours during the diagnostic. We'll have to manage ship's systems manually."

Nick shrugged. "Yes, but if it needs to be done, then so be it. We'll want every ship's system in full working order if we're going to launch a successful attack. We need certainty." Nick arched both eyebrows. "Agreed?"

"Yes, sir," said Gears, his lips forming a knowing grin. "I'll be on the flight deck and have the SIN off-line in two minutes." He hurried to the lift and was gone before the echo of his words had faded.

Nick turned to face Siren. "You'll have blasters and rifles fully charged for deployment?"

She nodded grimly.

"Bones, what about you?" Nick turned to look at the heavily muscled mercenary who had retrieved a blaster from the weapons locker recessed into the wall of the transportation bay and now had the pistol gripped in his right hand.

"I'll stun him if you tell me to," growled the big Martian-born man.

Nick grinned. "Okay. Good. We're ready."

Gears signaled from the flight deck that he had disabled the SIN.

I'm so glad they follow my train of thought no matter where it leads.

A beep from the materializer control console told them Tealmyn was ready for transport. "Okay, people, it's show time. Let's bring the man aboard."

11

BONES DIDN'T HAVE to stun Tealmyn, who
surrendered his weapons without an argument. He
didn't make any protest to his capture by Blaster
Squad; in fact, he didn't utter a single word when the
materializer beam released him to discover Bones
aiming a blaster at him.

Bones left the transportation bay via the lift, his
blaster pointed at the middle of Tealmyn's back. He
nodded to Nick as the lift doors closed. Tealmyn
would be in the quarantine room until the mission was
over.

The *Hunter* didn't have a jail for prisoners;
instead, they had a quarantine room where anyone
affected by some exotic infection or disease could be
held until they either discovered a cure or transported
them to a medical facility for treatment.

The room was about as escape proof as any jail. Nick was confidant Tealmyn wasn't going anywhere any time soon. Nick hoped the security chief's environmental suit had sufficient power to ensure their prisoner's comfort. He clearly wasn't in any mood to talk, but Nick didn't believe in torturing anyone needlessly.

"So what's next, boss?" said the Kid.

"After Bones gets back from tucking in our guest, we're going to transport to the surface. All except Gears, who'll be monitoring us from the flight deck." His eyes narrowed. "We may need a rapid extraction if things go sideways."

"Why did you disengage the SIN?" asked Siren, returning from the weapons locker where she had retrieved blast armor for all of them. Nick detected the scent of the oily polish designed to keep the armor clean and dry, even under the worst weather conditions imaginable.

Nick grunted. "I suspect our friend Tealmyn and his fellow Tuple are not only imposters but they are working for the Master. Gears told me the SIN was reprogrammed when the ship was upgraded and I suspect it has been clandestinely sending updates regarding our progress to someone. I didn't want it letting anyone know we'd changed the plan.

"I want them to think we're going to attack the Ferosians from orbit as planned."

"Why?" asked Bones, re-entering the bay through the lift doors. He handed each of them a field ration bar since none of them had eaten anything in a while. The bar tasted like chalk-flavored seaweed but it would provide them with the protein and vitamins they'd need to complete the mission.

Nick's lips formed a sardonic smile. "I think they want to start a war between the Ferosian factions and they want an attack by *aliens*—meaning us—to be the catalyst to start that war." He bit off a corner of the bar and swallowed rather than chewing it. *Real food would be nice. Too bad we don't have the time.* He barely tasted the musty seaweed flavor as it made its way down his throat. *Why hasn't the navy ever improved the taste of these things?*

The Kid's brow wrinkled. "So they destroy each other using the weapons supplied by the Master's spies, leaving the planet ripe for takeover." The younger man crossed his arms over his wide chest. "But what's in it for Tealmyn?"

Before Nick could speak, Siren handed the Kid his armor, then did the same to Bones and lastly Nick. As they slipped on their armor, she said,

"Tealmyn and his race will take a healthy percentage of the profits from the plunder of the Lestrom Nebula trade route."

"So these aliens, whoever they are, are pirates?" said the Kid.

"No, I don't think so. At least not in the traditional sense. I think they are mercenaries hired by the Master to prepare this planet for invasion. If they had attacked Feros III rather than this subterfuge, the Alliance would have been forced to act. In accordance with the Alliance Charter, a domestic dispute on a primitive world is not to be interfered with. The locals decide their own fate and the Alliance is unable by law to interfere."

Bones whistled softly. "Impressive. I like the subterfuge. "

Siren rolled her eyes, then said, "Have we notified the Alliance that these mercs are interfering with the Ferosians' development?"

"No. I don't have a lot of confidence in the Alliance right now. When Gears returned to the flight deck, he sent a prearranged coded message to Asia Call, who will lead a private task force of starships to rendezvous with us in orbit in five hours from now to defend this world."

"Are we expecting an attack?" asked Bones a little too eagerly.

Nick pursed his lips, his eyes scanning the faces of his squad. "I suspect when whoever is behind this infiltration of Feros III realizes what we're about to do, they'll send a fleet to destroy us and the Ferosians anyway."

Bones' eyes narrowed and he bit off a large piece of the bar and swallowed before speaking. ""I thought you said they didn't want to make an all-out attack, fearing the Alliance would stop them."

Nick nodded grimly. "Yes, I did, but they'll make a case that we are interfering and they have to stop *us* before *we* set off a war."

The Kid's eyes widened with realization. "So the fleet they'll send will be the Alliance Navy?"

Nick grinned. The Kid had good instincts. "Let's put on our light-absorbing jumpsuits and the armor. We need to get planet-side ASAP."

"What's asap?" asked the Kid.

Bones chuckled and clapped one massive hand on the younger man's shoulder. "Ya got a lot to learn, Kid, 'bout our old captain and his old-timey sayings."

12

IT WAS 0200 HOURS local time when Siren turned on a portable lamp, training the soft amber beam over the two thirty-meter-high steel doors secured by a padlocked steel crossbar sitting in brackets welded to the doors at the front of the massive weapons warehouse. The portable lamps were designed to emit just enough light to allow them to see their immediate surroundings, hopefully without attracting attention. The salt-tinged mist covered the ground as if they were walking on water. Thankfully the mist also helped to muffle their footsteps.

Nick could still taste the seaweed food ration bar; so could his stomach. It was like he'd swallowed a lump of lead.

101

In the distance he could see two guard towers and the electrified fence that surrounded the six hectares containing the six massive warehouses. Sensor scans of the area showed this complex was one of ten such facilities located near various cities on the continent. They were made to construct and store weapons. According to the sensor data, the other Ferosian continent had a similar number of warehouse complexes in concentrated areas much like this. The Ferosians were preparing themselves for a major war.

Searchlights on the watchtowers swept the areas beyond the fences, designed to detect an attack from an external direction. But the Ferosians didn't know about materializers, so they didn't expect Blaster Squad to transport inside their perimeter undetected.

Nick's heart beat quicker due to the rush of adrenaline he experienced when transporting into a potential area of conflict. His senses were on high alert for any signs of trouble. Looking at the faces of Bones, Siren, and the Kid, he saw they each had the same focused intensity as he felt. *Good.*

"Okay, everyone, let's blow this door and move inside," Nick said in a barely audible whisper into the wafer thin comm affixed to the strap over his left shoulder holding the chest plate of the blast armor in place.

The comm adjusted automatically to changes in decibel level and each team member had a miniature receiver in their ear. Stealth was critical to the success of the mission, so quiet was essential.

The Kid was the explosives expert so he stepped forward, slipped the pack off his back, and knelt on one knee next to one of the massive steel doors. He opened the pack and withdrew a small, three-square-centimeters of a fabric Gears had assured Nick was the newly designed implosive. The Kid had explained that this ordnance he and Gears had developed was called an implosion bomb. When affixed to an object by a strip of adhesive on one side of the fabric square, the bomb would be difficult if not impossible to remove or defuse. Once applied, all they had to do was send a predetermined signal to a microchip woven into the fabric to trigger the implosion.

When activated, the bomb became a miniature wormhole that would implode on itself and suck all matter within ten meters inward on itself, crushing it to dust instantly in total silence. Black holes swallow matter, light, sound, everything. Nick wondered if maybe this time Gears and the Kid had gone too far, but they assured him the miniature black hole would collapse very soon after the implosion. At least in theory.

After the bomb was ready, the Kid looked at Nick and nodded, his expression grim. Nick signaled they should all retreat to a safe distance thirty meters away. After they were hopefully far enough away, Nick indicated the Kid should proceed by making a twirling motion with his left index finger.

Nick waited for several seconds before moving until he realized he was holding his breath and let the air escape his lungs in a slow, shaky exhale. He hadn't felt fear in a long time but he recognized the perspiration dotting his brow, the tremors in his hands, and the knot of tension deep in his guts. He wasn't about to admit he was afraid but a look at the faces of his team told him they, too, were afraid. Most worrying was the Kid, who seemed uncertain about his and Gears' invention. Nick wondered if they'd had time to test the bomb, but somehow doubted it. Using untested weapons in the field was too often risky to life and limb.

No kidding, buddy, he thought sardonically. *At least I haven't lost my sense of self-deprecation.*

The Kid tapped his left wrist with two fingers and nothing happened. Nick began to wonder if this technology would work when the two doors and part of the roof high overhead suddenly disappeared as if they had never existed.

"That seemed to work pretty good," said Bones.

"*Well*," said Siren, correcting him, "it works *well*."

"Oh, look at her—the grammar police," growled Bones.

Nick smiled to himself. Releasing tension was different for everyone. Siren usually corrected Bones' grammatical errors and he pretended to hate it. It was their thing.

"Okay, everyone, let's move out. We have some weapons to implode." Nick spoke softly into his comm.

Nick crouched low and scampered toward the now open-air entrance to the warehouse. He had his blaster pistol in his right hand, ready in case they encountered any unexpected opposition. Sensor scans the Kid collected over several days of orbiting indicated the Ferosian security force conducted limited patrols at this time of the morning at this location. Nick hoped they'd be undisturbed while they took out the heavy weapons beyond that entrance.

"Fan out," he said, moving to the right side of the warehouse entrance. "Bones, take point."

The sounds of their boots running across the roadway were echoed by the now open entryway.

Siren stood with a blaster rifle on one side of the entrance, the portable lamp fixed to the barrel of the rifle. Bones stood in the middle with the Kid, their backs to each other, scanning the area for any threats. Nick was on the opposite side of the entrance to Siren.

"Clear," said Bones.

"Move inside," said Nick, his heart beating faster.

Slowly they moved inside as a group as if they were choreographed. Siren shifted the beam from the lamp to scan the area nearest them but it was empty. No weapons, no land vehicles, no guards, nothing. A growing sense of unease grew in Nick's belly with each step.

"Hey," said a feminine voice coming from their right, hidden in the deep shadows.

Nick recognized the voice immediately. He lowered his gun and stood fully erect. "Sonara Albright. What are you doing here?"

13

Outskirts of the city of Brexit
Military Warehouse Complex
Feros III
4150.11.5 Galactic

SONARA, SIREN'S SISTER, stepped from the shadows flanked by two tall, muscular mercenaries of the race who'd posed as Tuple. Each saurian held a plasma rifle, one aimed at Nick, the other at Bones. Nick's second in commands' sibling wore a sardonic grin on her angular features and her sky blue eyes sparkled with a look of smug confidence that Nick sorely wanted to blast off her face if the alien pirates hadn't got the drop on them.

On Sonara's right hip hung a large blaster pistol in a holster; on the other hip was a sheath holding a long, thin-bladed knife. Her shapely form was covered by a one-piece, skin hugging, ankle-to-neck suit made of a leather-like product.

And her shiny black hair was pulled into a ponytail that hung loosely halfway down her back. On her feet she wore sound absorbing boots that, as far as Nick knew, were only available to Alliance shock troopers. She stood with her long legs spread slightly apart and her arms crossed over her chest.

"You going to drop your weapons?"

Nick released his grip on his blaster until it fell, striking the floor with a smack, then skittering two meters away. Bones did the same as did the Kid, but Siren glared at Sonara, her rifle aimed at her sister, the beam from the lamp surrounding Sonara's head like a halo. But Nick knew Sonara was no saint. She switched sides every time the wind changed direction.

Sonara uncrossed her arms, then took a step closer to Siren, one hand on the butt of the blaster still in her holster. "What 'bout you, my dear sis?" She arched an eyebrow, her expression one of challenge.

Slowly Nick saw Siren's grip loosen on the rifle, then she flipped it, the butt end facing away from her causing the guards to shift their aim to her. She chuckled grimly, then stepped toward Sonara and handed her the butt of the rifle. "There you go, you lying sack of crap." She arched both thin eyebrows, her eyes flaring with burning anger. "Happy?"

If looks could melt you where you stood, these two would be puddles of goo, thought Nick.

Sonara offered her sister a mirthless smile as she accepted the offered weapon. As she walked past him with Siren's rifle cradled in her arms, Nick detected the faint odor of cinnamon coming from her.

"What's going on, Sonara?" asked Nick.

Sonara handed the rifle to one of her guards, then turned to face him. Her eyes were devoid of emotion but her lips had formed a mirthless smile. Frankly, her expression creeped him out. "You were going to disrupt our plans." She looked away and cleared her throat as if she was struggling with some hidden anger. "We had no choice but to stop you…ask you to transport back to your ship to continue with the planned bombardment."

Form the corner of one eye, Nick noticed Siren's features were flushed and her hands had curled into fists at her sides. Nick arched an eyebrow and crossed his arms over his chest plate. A trickle of perspiration ran down his back beneath his jumpsuit. "How did you detect us?"

"We knew you were coming," Sonara said, her eyes shifting from him to Siren and back again.

"How could you?" said Bones. "We captured your man…"

Sonara snorted. "That solider has already been terminated along with your pilot. The Master's plan will be realized and this world will be cleared of the weak and backward life forms so we can occupy it."

"Who is *we* exactly?" asked Nick, though his mind was reeling concerning the possibility Gears had been killed; he needed to stay focused. "The Alliance? The Master? These mercenaries?" He glared at the two saurian guards, making a slight nod of his head. Anger burned in his belly.

"We are *not* mercenaries," growled one of the guards, who directed his rifle at Nick; its eyes burned with resentment. Nick detected the increase in the odor of slime in the air, which suggested he had gotten a rise out of the alien mercenary. Of course, the blaster aimed at his chest was a pretty clear indicator as well.

Sonara approached the guard and placed a hand on the barrel of his rifle; she pressed down to lower the barrel. "Don't fall for Captain Justice's tricks. He's trying to distract you so his team can overpower you." Her eyes smiled at Nick. "Isn't that right, *Captain*?"

Nick tried to swallow but his mouth was dry. "You know me well," he said, his voice a hoarse whisper.

Sonara chuckled sarcastically. "Of course. My sister told me a lot about you, Nick. I know exactly how Blaster Squad operates, and how your compassion and empathy make you weak. I plan to exploit this weakness for the advantage of my Master." Her eyes narrowed. "After we conquer the galaxy, there may even be a spot for you." She laughed mirthlessly, eyeing him suggestively causing him to cringe. "Perhaps as my personal slave."

Siren—who up to now had let her sister rant on without objecting—snorted derisively, causing Sonara to glare at her. "Really, my *dear* sister, since when did you care about politics?" spat Siren. "All you've ever cared about is the accumulation of wealth and personal gain. You've never fought for a cause in your life."

"Times change," growled Sonara. "People, too."

Siren emitted a bark of laughter and shook her head.

"We have to get back, Centurion," said one of the guards. "The Master is expecting a progress report."

Sonara's angular, pale features relaxed as the anger disappeared from her eyes. "Yes, Vruor, quite right."

"What about us?" said Nick, unable to keep his defiance from his voice.

Sonara looked thoughtful, her brow creased, her eyes narrow for several seconds. "I was planning to kill you all but I think I'll wait for later when I have more time. I want you all to suffer before you die." She shrugged. "No quick deaths for you, I'm afraid, because the Master has a job for you to complete."

"We are *not* going to bombard the Ferosians," Nick said.

Sonara offered him a sardonic smile and her eyes flared slightly. "Would you prefer a slow, painful death for you and your crew, or a quick and easy one?" Nick didn't respond; instead he glared at her. She grunted. "No worries, Nick. If you don't care about that, how about I torture your crew and kill them each slowly one by one while you watch?"

Nick's cheeks became warm and he clenched his fists tighter, his guts twisted with fury. *I'll make her pay dearly if she harms my friends.*

He was about to take his chances and lunge at her when, behind the guards, a doorway opened through which daylight poured into the darkened warehouse. The sun had come up. Shielding his eyes from the sudden intrusion of bright light through the portal or doorway, Nick could see an expansive green field dotted with white, red, and blue flowers. In the distance was an Alliance shuttle.

112

Several saurian mercenaries were visible near the opening on the other side. They were armed with the same plasma rifles as the two guards. Their coal black eyes were intent on what had to be the portal Gears had described to Nick earlier. This was obviously technology far beyond the materializer.

Plasma rifles, Alliance shuttles, a type of teleporter far beyond their own technology, sound absorbing boots only issued to Alliance Shock Troops, alien mercenaries, and now Sonara Albright shows up…what was going on here? How far did the reach of this so-called Master go?

Nick scowled at Sonara as she signaled for them to enter the portal. Bones glanced at Nick and he could see the big man's uncertainty. "It's okay, Bones. I don't think they're going to kill us, at least not now."

Bones stepped through, followed quickly by Siren and the Kid. They disappeared and Nick couldn't see them on the other side. He hesitated thinking maybe Sonara had killed them after all. "Sonara, where are they?"

"On your ship, of course," she said matter-of-factly.

14

GSS Hunter
Orbiting Feros III
4150.11.5 Galactic

NICK STEPPED THROUGH the portal onto the flight
deck of the *Hunter* to find his crew seated at their
usual stations. He froze for a second, surprised he
wasn't in a green field surrounded by an army of
alien mercs, but relieved to be home. Looking at his
surroundings, he saw Siren at engineering, the Kid
at sensors, and Bones at weapons, all of them intent
on their station's screens. The only one missing was
Gears, who was absent from the pilot's station, giving
Nick a sinking feeling the tech genius may have
indeed been killed as Sonara claimed.

What the heck is going on?

"Siren. What's happening?" asked Nick, moving
to the copilot's station where he sat in the chair.

"We're monitoring a fleet of Alliance ships entering the system, sir," she said, her eyes flitting back and forth across the screen in front of her. "Gears, how's it going down there?"

Nick heart seemed to skip a beat. *He's alive?* His eyes drifted to Tealmyn, who was also very much alive, contrary to what Sonara told him. Nick decided he should check the systems at his station before asking any more questions. He desperately needed information, but his crew appeared consumed with something he sensed was important and they needed to do their jobs right now rather than be interrupted with a lot of questions.

But Nick wasn't sure he'd actually transported aboard his own vessel. Nothing he'd seen or heard so far seemed to make much sense. *I* really *need to figure this out.*

He brought up the propulsion reports on the center screen in front of him. The power levels were adequate but not up to full power. He checked the flight control system's report on the screen to the right of the middle one and everything seemed ready to go. "Kid, transfer your sensor readings of that inbound fleet to my delta screen."

The three screens at each station were designated alpha, beta, and delta; alpha, or A, for the screen on the left side of the operator's station; beta, or B, for the center screen; and finally delta, or D, being the screen on the right side of the operator's station. This avoided any confusion about which screen they were referring to.

"Aye, Captain, you should have them on your D screen now," said the Kid.

Does the Kid think we've suddenly become pirates? "Thanks, Kid," said Nick.

The data from the long-range sensors showed the incoming fleet consisted of three massive battlewagons armed with sixteen banks of plasma cannons and a larger number of blaster cannons, five heavily armed heavy cruisers, and fifty picket ships to guard the perimeter of the fleet. No doubt the battlewagons also carried planet busters. These were specially designed ordnance to drill into the planet's crust until they reached the core, where they'd explode and cause massive quakes literally shaking the planet apart. A terrible weapon of mass destruction.

Nick eased back in his chair, his mood now dark and sullen. Somehow they had to stop the Alliance fleet without dying themselves.

The problem was they were as out-gunned as a primitive with a slingshot. They wouldn't last more than a few seconds under the guns of that fleet and he didn't relish the idea of death just yet.

"What's Gears doing?" Nick asked to no one in particular.

He heard the lift arriving at the rear of the flight deck. Spinning his chair around, Nick watched Gears exit the lift car and head for the pilot's chair. He wanted to grab the smaller man and hug the stuffing out of him, but since the tech genius wasn't overly comfortable with public displays of affection, he suppressed the urge. *Hug the stuffing out of him? Boy, my great-granny's phrases really sound ridiculous, even to me. Best leave that one in my head.*

A sense of relief washed over him until he realized Tealmyn was also alive, meaning Sonara had lied about killing them. But why? And who was she lying to? It didn't make sense she'd lie to them since they'd quickly discover the lie. Nick had the sense something far more intricate was at work here.

"Gears," Nick said, "what were you doing?"

"I needed to put a software patch into the Systems Information Network's fluidic memory core so we could reactivate it." He lowered his voice.

"We need the SIN if we're going to survive the next few hours. I may be a great pilot, but I can't make the maneuvers we'll need against that fleet out there by myself."

"Did it work?"

Gears nodded. "It's not a permanent fix, it won't last long. I need the facilities of the Armstrong Shipyard in Earth orbit to complete the work properly, but we don't have time to get there and back before the Alliance fleet arrives."

"Stating the obvious again, *Gearhead*?" said the Kid sardonically.

Gears chuckled coldly. "Somebody has to muscle head."

Nick waited for the Kid's usual retort, but when he didn't say anything, Nick swiveled his chair to look at the younger man. The Kid's mouth hung open; staring at his screen, his eyes were wide and his usually tanned features were as pale as if he'd seen a ghost.

"Kid, you need some water?" asked Siren from her station.

"Huh, no. Thanks. Everyone, look at your B screen," said the Kid, his eyes confused.

Nick's brain didn't immediately register what he was seeing.

118

Then his mouth dried and his heart skipped a beat as he recognized a massive space/time displacement wave entering from the opposite direction of the approaching Alliance fleet. It meant someone was entering the system with their FTL drive fully engaged. The wave would disrupt comets and asteroids, scattering them across the system in wild trajectories. No doubt some of those displaced comets and asteroids would strike some or all of the eight worlds in this system, causing untold destruction and death.

Planets would be thrown off their axes, resulting in tidal waves, earthquakes, shifts in magnetic fields and gravity. Millions of beings would die.

What do I do? Nick wondered as his guts knotted in terror.

15

THE EMERGENCY ALARM echoed across the flight deck, making clear-headed thinking difficult. The lights had dimmed to battle mode, so everything and everyone had a soft amber glow and the screens at every station were brighter.

"What do I do, sir?" yelled Gears, snapping Nick back into reality.

"Sir, the Alliance fleet has gone to emergency FTL! They have exited the system ahead of the wave," the Kid shouted from his station.

Nick looked at his B screen and saw that the space/time displacement wave seemed to have slowed. It took several seconds for this change to register as significant. "Gears! All of you, be quiet and look at the screen! And shut off that alarm!"

The alarm ended abruptly. Nick swallowed hard, then said, "Gears, what's happening to the displacement wave?"

"I don't know, Captain, I've never seen anything like it. The wave has dissipated and I have no idea how."

Nick shifted his gaze to the tech genius who had an amazed expression on his face that made his stomach tighten. He had never seen Gears so confused it was unsettling.

"Sir, " interrupted Siren drawing his attention away from Gears. Nick spun his chair toward his second in command at the engineering station. "There's an incoming message." She paused, her features intent on listening. "It's Asia Call." She paused again and her brow wrinkled in concentration. "The message is faint due to distance…" Her voice trailed off. Then she continued. "She says her fleet is in a battle with a pirate fleet three light years from here in the Hynug system. She said she was the one who sent the disruption wave and hoped it helped." She paused again, her eyes reflecting a rush of worry in her voice. "The message ends abruptly."

"Do you have a fix on her location?" asked Nick.

Without a sensor fix within a system, it was like hunting for an opossum in a field of tall grass—in other words, virtually impossible.

Siren nodded. "She's near the sixth planet in the system, a gas giant."

Gears instructed the repaired SIN to bring up a chart of the Hynug system on the tri-screens in the center of the flight deck. The screens lit up and Nick saw there were eighteen planets in the system. "SIN, magnify the sixth planet for us."

The image on the screen shifted so he could see the ten moons orbiting a rust-red planet. On one side of the screen were the statistics for this gas giant. Like most planets of this class, it was a failed star; but this one had an iron core denser than most, giving it a strong magnetic field causing massive gravity fluctuations. Navigating the eddies and swirls of unstable gravity during a battle was quite a feat of piloting. No wonder Asia's signal was weaker than normal for only being three light years from the Feros system. No doubt even the moons orbiting the planet and any stray asteroids would be unstable and have misshapen orbits in this volatile system. The place was as close to a pilot's worst nightmare as any he'd ever encountered in his travels. And they were going there.

16

GSS Hunter
Hynug system
4150.11.8 Galactic

THEY'D COME OUT of FTL two hours ago. Since that time, Nick and the Kid had been trying to make sense of the confusing sensor readings coming from the Hynug system. At .99 light speed, they would come within range of Asia's ship in the next twenty-three minutes. Nick expected she was using the *Survivor,* but her message a few days ago had said something about a fleet of ships.

Nick took a long drink from the bottle of vitamin water Siren had provided them after they left the hyper-sleep pods. He swallowed the cool, lemon-flavored beverage, then said, "Kid, see any ships in this mess?" He was growing increasingly frustrated by the lack of solid information about what to expect.

"Yes, boss, but the readings are fragmented due to the gravity and magnetic fluctuations coming from the area of the sixth planet. It's sending waves of hyper-magnetism across the system, confusing our scans. I'm not sure how our stealth shields will react to this environment."

"How many ships are there?" Nick persisted. He knew they were facing a dangerous environment in addition to pirates but he needed to know what they were up against.

"I count fifteen ships of various sizes and armaments, as far as I can tell from the readings." The Kid snorted in frustration. "But I can't be sure. It might be fifteen hundred or it might be five. With the fluctuation in these readings, I can't tell with absolute certainty."

He spun his chair toward Nick. He looked haggard and tired, the corners of his eyes drooping and heavy dark circles under them. The Kid had been alone on the ship while they were on Feros III and he had been working hard to provide Nick with as much information as possible. Even the time spent in the hyper-sleep pod didn't seem to have helped him relax. Of course, in hyper-sleep you don't actually sleep. It's more like lost time than restful. Your mind can be very active during hyper-sleep.

Nick lowered his voice. "It's okay, Kid, just give me your best guess." He shrugged. "The truth is, we'll all find out together when we get there anyway."

The Kid gave him a weak smile in response and Nick patted his back, then headed back to the copilot's station. He sat down with a sharp exhale of breath, causing Gears to glance at him. He didn't like this situation at all; he felt vulnerable when he didn't have control.

"Well, sir," said the tech genius, "we going in or not?"

Nick nodded. "Of course we are, Gears, and you know better than anyone we have to."

Gears knew, if Nick decided to enter a fight, it was something worth fighting for. And where Asia Call was concerned, Nick had always been there to provide backup for his mentor when she needed him. She took him in after a gang of saboteurs murdered his family when he was still a teenager. Nick had vowed to bring the criminals to justice, but in the past thirty years he hadn't even come close to finding those responsible. It was Nick's one regret, but someday he would find them and make them pay for leaving him an orphan.

"Captain," said Siren, interrupting his thoughts. "We should engage the stealth shields soon or someone might notice us. We've seen far too much advanced tech on this mission to discount the possibility of being detected even in this volatile environment."

Nick knew she was right. He took the last sip of vitamin water from the bottle, then swallowed. "She's right, Gears, engage the stealth shields."

Gears eased forward slightly in his chair and pressed the activation icon on the screen in the center of his station. His brow furrowed. "That's odd," he muttered. "SIN, why didn't the shields engage?"

"They did," replied the System Information Network.

"Uh, no, SIN, they did not."

The AI paused in a very human manner. "My system diagnostics suggest they did engage but were quickly shut down by an external force. The reaction time was less than a millisecond, insufficient time for the sensors to report the error. I now have the error on record."

"*How comforting*," piped up Bones sarcastically.

"What external force was involved…describe it for us," said Gears, his anxious voice making Nick edgy. Something had gone very wrong.

126

The SIN spoke in dulcet tones as if nothing out the ordinary was happening. "There is a vessel in high orbit of the seventh planet in the system. It is transmitting waves of disruptive energy to encompass the entire system. This class of energy disrupts communication and interferes with protective screens and other ship's systems."

"Sir," snapped Siren, her tense voice making Nick's heart beat faster. "The containment field around the FTL drive is failing…and the sublight drive is also failing. The safety protocols will shut the engines down before the protection grid reaches critical. We're going to be dead in space in the next ten minutes if we don't do something. Fast."

"Bones," said Nick, "can you get a fix on that ship?" The big man nodded. "Then target that ship using the data from the Kid's sensors and fire plasma torpedoes, full spread…Do it now. We don't have much time."

Just as Bones fired the torpedoes, the lights on the flight deck flickered and the amber emergency lighting came on to conserve power. The constant hum of the engines coming through the deck plating beneath his feet suddenly ceased as the emergency shutdown of the engine core activated in order to not overload and blow them into atoms.

Screens around the room went dark as they lost power. The room became warmer and Nick felt the tickle of sweat running down his forehead. Soon the gravity stabilizers would fail and the air would become stale. Finally the emergency lighting would quit and they'd be helpless on a dying ship.

Without engines, they'd drift on their current course forever as life support systems failed until the gravity of the system's sun dragged them in and they became one with the superheated gases that fuel a star. Not that this mattered; without air regenerators and scrubbers, they'd be dead long before they fell into the star.

Nick didn't relish the idea of freezing and suffocating before being turned into charcoal. The ship shuddered as gravity waves emanating from the sixth planet washed over the *Hunter*. *Maybe we'll shake apart before we suffocate or before we cook. One has to stay optimistic*, he mused.

After what seemed like forever, the ship's amber emergency lights flickered again, then steadied as the lighting changed back to normal. The whirr of the air vents opening could be heard as the regenerators kicked in to clear the air of the increased carbon dioxide from their breathing.

This coupled with the workstation screens coming to life once again at the crew stations made Nick realize he too often took the normal sights, sounds, and smells of everyday ship operations for granted. The sour smell of sweat filled his nostrils. *That's never going to happen again*, he thought as the tension between his shoulder blades decreased.

"Kid, any readings?" Nick gasped, his voice hoarse from lack of breathable air.

The Kid coughed to clear his lungs, then said, "Good news and bad news, sir. The good news is the disruptive waves have ceased. The bad news is the ship in orbit around the seventh planet is only disabled. I'm reading their power grid is still fully operational, though at somewhat lower levels than before. Our torpedoes must have been slightly off target, but at least they knocked them out of action for now."

"We better get outta here fast before they get that weapon back online," said Bones. "Great job, Kid."

Nick grinned at Bones' compliment of the Kid's report, then turned his attention to Siren's station and saw her sprawled on the deck, lying on her side. Her eyes were closed and she didn't appear to be breathing.

A cut on her forehead where she'd struck the console on her way down was still bleeding, meaning her heart was still pumping.

No! He rushed to kneel beside her. Taking her right wrist between his thumb and index finger, he checked for a pulse and was relieved when he found one; but it was very faint. *What the hell happened*?

17

GSS Hunter
Hynug system
4150.11.8 Galactic

"SIN, TRANSPORT SIREN to a stasis pod in the
medical bay and start the resuscitation protocol."
Nick stood and took a step back from his second
in command's unconscious body on the deck and
watched as she shimmered in the glow of the
materializer, then disappeared.

"She gonna be okay?" asked Bones. Nick glanced
at the muscular Martian human hybrid still at the
weapons station and offered him a sharp nod in reply.

"We have to get to Asia and find out what's going
on." His eyes travelled around the worried faces of
his remaining crew. "The future of the galaxy is at
stake." Nick softened his tone. "I'm worried about her
too, but unless we stop the Master, she—and likely
we all—will be dead soon.

"I'm sure the stasis pod will keep her among the living until we reach a qualified medical tech." Nick was unconvinced himself about this last statement but he had to believe it to sell it to his team.

Bones, Gears, and the Kid nodded in unison, their expressions serious.

"Okay, Kid, what readings are you getting from those ships in the area of the sixth planet?"

"The readings have stabilized; now that we're close enough to read them, I'm showing only three ships are operational and still have viable life support. All three are heavily damaged and their engines and weapons are off-line."

That doesn't sound good, thought Nick. "How long until we get within materializer range?" The *Hunter* shuddered as if it had struck something, except the navigational shields would have absorbed a hit by any debris and deflected the energy from any strike.

"Two minutes, sir," said Gears.

The deck beneath them trembled and Gears assumed manual control, his face flushed with the exertion of maintaining their course as he struggled with the control stick.

He pressed two icons on his B screen, focusing his attention on the image on the screen of the three ships being tossed about in gravity waves as if they were corks on a rough sea.

"Life forms?" Nick asked as the *Hunter* seemed to skid sideways in a gravity eddy requiring the gravity compensators to quickly make an adjustment so they didn't shoot to the ceiling. His stomach heaved and he tasted sour bile at the back of his throat.

"I'm reading two indistinct life forms, sir," said the Kid. "On one of the vessels. The other two ships have been penetrated by meteorites and other debris and have lost their atmospheres. Their power plants are still operating on minimal levels but they are devoid of life. One vessel still has limited shielding but that appears about to fail."

"Gears, get us as close as you can to that ship containing the life forms," said Nick, gritting his teeth as the *Hunter* groaned and creaked around them. The stresses of the gravity and tidal waves of energy that were pounding them would eventually disable their shields. Nick mentally crossed his fingers, hoping they'd make it out of here before they were like the other ships in orbit of the sixth planet.

"It's the *Survivor!*" shouted Gears. "Asia Call's ship."

Nick eyes locked on the screen as Gears increased magnification until he could see the white hull of Asia's ship, which was now blackened and scarred, and sections of hull plating were missing. After seeing its condition, the fact the *Survivor* had any atmosphere at all seemed remarkable.

"Can you get a fix on those life forms?" Nick asked, the knot in his stomach growing tighter.

"Yes, sir," said the Kid.

"Gears, can you lock on with the materializer?"

"Got 'em," said Gears between gritted teeth.

"Two beings transported aboard," said the SIN. "They are in the transportation bay."

"Sir!" shouted Gears. "We have to get out of here now. The plasma fuel containment tanks on all three of those ships are about to rupture. If we don't get out of range of the explosions, not even our shielding will protect us from a blast of that magnitude."

"How long?" asked Nick, uncertain he really wanted the answer.

"We have ten minutes," said Gears.

18

THE *HUNTER* DROPPED out of FTL and slowed, using its navigation thrusters until it was drifting in the solar winds coming from the Feros star. The hyper-sleep pods began the cycle to awaken their occupants. The lid to Nick's pod opened and he sat up, feeling slightly sick in the pit of his stomach.

That was too close for comfort, he thought as his mind cleared. Blinking away the sleep from his eyes, he puffed out his cheeks, then blew air from his lungs. His throat and mouth were dry, so after he stood on the deck of the hyper-sleep pod bay, he went to the hydration dispenser and selected a bottle of lemon vitamin water. He would need to balance his electrolytes as quickly as possible if he was going to be in any shape to complete the mission.

No doubt Gears would select his usual banana flavor, the Kid his T-bone steak-flavored water, and Bones his blood sausage water. Nick cringed when the Kid and Bones asked that these flavors of vitamin water be kept in stock. He had never tried them but they sounded nauseating. *To each his own*, Nick mused. *No matter how disgusting.*

He glanced at Siren, who had already emerged from her pod and was still dressed in her flight suit—they hadn't had a chance to change into hyper-jumpsuits given the urgency of the jump—as she approached from his right and took a bottle of jasmine-green tea infused vitamin water for herself. Nick was more than pleased to see her after she'd struck her head and blacked out during battle in the Hynug system.

When they had found Asia and a Lobsan warrior unconscious on the deck of the transportation bay, they had moved them to the medical bay only to discover Siren, revived and asking what happened and why she was in the medical bay. Nick quickly explained the larger problem.

After sealing Asia and the alien warrior in medical pods, with seconds to spare before the three ships in orbit around the sixth planet exploded.

They were sealed in hyper-sleep pods when the SIN engaged the FTL drive just as the massive blast wave of super-heated plasma reached their position. Blaster Squad had narrowly escaped death once again. Nick wondered how many more times this would be true before their luck ran dry.

Gears came up beside them and grabbed a bottle of the banana flavor as Nick expected he would. He opened it and drained half the bottle before speaking. "I do not want to make another jump without a jumpsuit any time soon."

"You got that right," agreed Siren before she tipped up her open bottle and drained it in one go.

They both took another bottle of water and headed for the lift, which he had already seen the Kid take to the flight deck. Youngest to join, first to recover. *I must be getting old.*

"Where're you going?" asked Nick. "You okay?"

She shrugged. "I'm going to the medical bay to check on our patients and…" she shifted her gaze briefly to Gears, "I suspect my pal here is going to the flight deck to conduct a systems check. We'll wanna be ready to take on whatever we find back at Feros III."

Nick grinned and Gears nodded, with a brief smile passing between them.

Nick opened the second bottle and took a swig just as the lift doors closed and Gears and Siren disappeared.

Bones came up beside him. "Hey, Cap, how long's it gonna take to get to Feros III? I *really* wanna kick me some tushie."

Nick stifled a grin. No need to encourage this guy.

"Captain." Siren's voice came over the comm. Nick sensed tension in her tone.

"What's up?" Nick replied.

"Asia and her…" she hesitated and Nick could barely make out a woman's gentle voice, which he knew very well, speaking from somewhere nearby. "…second are awake and want to talk to you."

"Okay, I'll be right there." Nick cut off the comm and shrugged at Bones, who grunted. "Duty calls, big guy. You go to the bridge and tell Gears and the Kid to set course for Feros III. Get us underway as soon as possible at .99 light speed."

"Aye, aye, sir," said Bones with a sardonic grin.

Nick rolled his eyes at the tech's use of navy lingo, then took the last swig of the lemon-flavored water and swallowed. He then tossed the empty bottle in the recycler where it would broken down to its base components, then reconstituted into other items. Nothing was ever wasted on a starship.

He entered the lift car and instructed it to take him to the medical bay. The door closed on a haggard looking Bones still grinning at him. *We'll all need a long holiday after this, my friend.*

He exited the lift car as it arrived at the medical bay to find a scowling Siren, her long arms folded across her chest. "What's the matter?" asked Nick.

"It's me. Sorry."

Nick shifted his gaze from his second in command to discover Asia standing, one hand on a medical pod, looking as bad as he felt. Her normally healthy features were drawn and gray and one leg appeared to have been broken and was secured by an old-fashioned splint.

"She refused to accept my help to mend her leg until you got here," Siren said bitterly. "She's as stubborn as an old man riding into town on a mule." Nick opened his mouth to correct her mixing up of two old sayings but decided it could wait.

Asia arched an eyebrow. "What have you been teaching this woman?"

Nick chuckled grimly. "Never mind. Let her help you while you tell me what's so important."

Asia nodded and nearly fainted, but Siren rushed to her side and helped her onto a treatment bed.

The treatment screen projected from the side of the bed and moved upward until it locked in place. The screen was set at a forty-five-degree angle so Siren could enter instructions and so she could read the data as the bed scanned Asia for injuries. The creases on Siren's forehead deepened as she studied the data. "I have a lot to do here," she said softly. Nick knew this meant she wouldn't be talking much for a while.

"So tell me, Asia," said Nick as he moved to stand beside the bed.

Asia swallowed and her eyes glazed over a bit as the treatment bed injected painkillers into her bloodstream. "The Master is behind everything that's happened."

Nick listened intently, taking her hand in his to comfort her as Siren began to work on her injuries. In a steady voice, Asia began to explain how the Master used pirates, financed by his new empire's backers, to steal the advanced weapons they'd seen on Feros III. The weapons had been stolen from an Alliance research planet near the outer rim of the galaxy. The council kept the thefts secret, fearing the existence of such weapons would attract criminal elements throughout the galaxy like flies to honey.

Nick smiled to himself at her mix-up of another ancient saying.

She continued by telling him she was on the way to Feros III with a fleet of fifteen warships gathered from various non-aligned worlds when they received a distress signal from the Hynug system. Galactic law required any passing vessel to respond to a distress call, so they made the course correction.

When they entered the Hynug system, their comms were immediately jammed and soon their weapons and shields went off-line. A larger fleet of pirate vessels attacked just as most of Asia's fleet became vulnerable.

Asia's engineer and those from two other vessels managed to engage the sublight engines, weapons, and partial shields so they survived the initial onslaught of enemy ships while the rest of her fleet was destroyed. Before this happened, they had managed to take out ten of the pirate ships before entering the dangerous space around the sixth planet in order to hide from their attackers. The remaining pirates abandoned the attack and disappeared, or at least that's what their instruments said.

"So what can we expect at Feros III?" Nick asked her, squeezing her hand gently.

Before she could respond, Nick felt the deck beneath his feet tremble. His senses went on high alert and the knot of tension between his shoulder blades returned with a vengeance. "Gears, what's going on?" he said.

"We're under attack, sir, by a ship of unknown design. It's armed with plasma cannons and something else," Gears responded. "They're firing plasma cannons but our defensive screens are holding. Their ship is too far away for their weapons to be completely effective."

"What's the something else?" asked Nick with a growing sense of unease. The tech genius was avoiding the subject. How could things get any worse?

Over the comm, he heard Gears sigh. "They have a device I'm pretty sure generates a time/space displacement wave like the one we detected a few days ago in the Feros system."

Oh, crap. "How long have we got until they fire the thing at us?"

"I'm guessing, sir," responded Gears, "but the sensor data confirms they are in the process of cycling the weapon to full power and I'd say they will fire inside fifteen minutes.

Before you ask, the leading edge of the wave will strike us ten minutes after they fire. Not long after that…well, sir, you get the idea."

Nick pondered the problem since he did indeed get the idea all too clearly. He said, "Are we within weapons range?"

"Not yet, but we will be before they fire the weapon."

So it's fight or flight, thought Nick. He grunted. They were going to make a stand here and now. They would fight. Even if it meant they'd die.

19

NICK ENTERED THE flight deck with Asia beside him to find Gears, the Kid, and Bones busy at their stations. They left Asia's second in the medical bay. He'd injured one of his four arms and would require surgery to fix it.

Gears had turned over piloting duties to the SIN since he was busy concentrating on the Kid's sensor readings.

Nick smiled to himself. Gears preferred to pilot the *Hunter* manually, treating the ship as if it were his child. Turning over control to the AI was quite a sacrifice for the tech genius. Nick directed his mentor to sit at the engineering station while he slipped into the copilot's seat just as Gears made a surprising report.

"Sir," said Gears before Nick could issue orders, "a second ship has appeared. It was in stealth mode until now."

Nick glanced at Asia, but if he was reading her correctly, she had no idea who this might be. Still, he knew she had the ability to hide her thoughts from him by betraying nothing through her eyes or on her face like most people. She was a great poker player.

"The new arrival is attacking the other ship, raking it with plasma cannons and blasters. The first ship has turned to repel the attack. It's no longer directing fire at us."

"Put the image of those ships on the tri-screen." He looked at Gears. "Get us within weapons range." He shifted his gaze to Bones. "Don't fire until I tell you." He paused and waited until Bones nodded he understood. Nick wasn't going to let Bones misconstrue his orders. Not this time.

Nick swiveled his chair toward the tri-screen closest to him as they flickered to life, then steadied, showing the two vessels locked in combat firing plasma cannons at each other across the darkness of space. Beams of intense, superheated energy lashed out at each other. The brilliant indigo rays struck each vessel's defensive screens, making them glow as the shields struggled to absorb the highly charged energy.

Nick wondered if he should intervene. It clearly made sense to attack the strange looking craft with its swept wings and bulbous mound that ran down the middle between the wings since it had been attacking them before the second vessel appeared. Rows of plasma cannons sticking from the wings fireding continuously as it tried unsuccessfully to maneuver to avoid the other ship's fire. The strange craft had a large, scoop-shaped cone at one end of the elongated, gleaming gray hull he assumed was the space/time disruption weapon.

The second vessel's design had more in common with many pirate vessels he had seen before. It was blocky-shaped with four large engine exhaust ports at the rear. A small bump at the opposite end from the exhaust ports indicated this was the flight deck. Outside zero-G atmospheres, spacecraft don't have to be beautiful to be an efficient design. And from the growing intensity of the glow of the first vessel's screens, their shields were overloading. The image of the two ships on the screen grew larger with each passing second as they drew closer to the battle.

They both better get out of there before they're in serious trouble, thought Nick.

"Nick," said Asia from the engineering station. "There's a signal coming in from the pirate ship."

She looked into his eyes with one eyebrow arched. "It's Sonara Albright."

Nick's cheeks cooled as blood drained from his face. *Sonara*? "Okay," he said slowly from between gritted teeth. "Open the channel. Everyone needs to hear what she has to say."

She had created havoc and put their lives at risk during their time on Brimstone V, so this conversation would be a difficult one. He was convinced Sonara had caused the Alliance Navy to wipe out the inhabitants of the mining world just as she escaped in a private starship. Now here she was again. His eyes flitted to Asia. There had to be a connection.

"Hello, Sonara," Nick began, struggling to keep the anger and disgust from his voice, "what is your situation?"

"Nick. So good to hear your voice. Is my sister with you?"

"Yes," he said curtly.

"Our plasma fuel tank has been ruptured so I don't have much time. Sirenna, I'm so sorry if I hurt you. I had to do this. I had no choice. Asia can tell you."

Nick glared at his mentor. Just as he suspected, she was up to her arched eyebrows in this mess. Asia cringed, her eyes avoiding him.

"Gears, how long until we're within materializer range?"

Before the tech genius could respond, the Kid said, "Sir, I'm reading a massive buildup in the fuel tanks on both ships. Hold on," he added as he sucked in a breath. "According to these readings, we have two minutes to get out of range before the explosion engulfs us. I doubt our shields will deflect enough of the radiation." His eyes widened. "Both the alien ships' shields have failed."

"Gears," said Nick. "Transport every life form you can get a lock on aboard Sonara's vessel here. Then get us out of here at maximum sublight speed!"

Gears mouth formed a grim line and his fingers flew across the control screen, pressing various icons until he shouted at the AI. "SIN, transport them now!"

Just as Gears uttered his last syllable, the two alien ships on the screen erupted in orange, yellow, and blue fireballs as their tanks, filled with highly explosive plasma, breached and exploded on contact with what air remained in the ships' engine rooms. The *Hunter*'s sublight engine was engaged and the blast wave of deadly radiation grew steadily smaller and smaller on the screen until it was a bright pinpoint of light, then finally disappeared altogether. But Nick knew it wasn't gone.

The radiation wave would slowly dissipate and lose its strength as the charged particles moved away from each other until it became no more deadly that background radiation. Until then, it was dangerous to humanoid life.

"SIN? Did we get them?" said Nick anxiously.

"One life form has been transported aboard," replied the AI's calm voice.

Nick scanned the bridge. "Siren, you're with me. The rest of you, continue to monitor that radiation wave and let me know where it's headed. And I want options if it's headed for Feros III." Bones, Gears, and the Kid acknowledged the orders with grim expressions on their sleep-deprived faces. Asia continued to avoid his gaze.

Nick rose and walked to the lift, with Siren right behind him. They entered the lift together, not looking at each other or uttering a word. "Transportation bay," Nick said before the lift doors closed.

"You okay?" Nick asked Siren, who had closed her eyes and leaned her head back. Her back rested against the wall of the lift car.

"Not really," she said. She opened her eyes and leaned her head forward; her eyes were glassy. "What about Asia?"

"What about her?" said Nick, the bitterness in his voice as sharp as a finely honed knife blade.

"Obviously Sonara is working with her."

Nick nodded. "Yeah. Obviously." The lift doors opened to reveal Sonara, dressed neck to toe in blast armor holding a plasma rifle, which she pointed at them. She didn't have a helmet on and her long hair draped over her shoulders. She wore a sardonic grin on her angular features and her blues eyes sparked with arrogance.

Nick grunted. "Nothing ever changes with you," he muttered.

20

NICK STEPPED OUT of the lift car with a derisive smirk on his lips. "Hello, Sonara, nice to see you survived."

Sonara used the plasma rifle to wave him to her left to stand against the wall. Nick did as directed but his eyes remained locked on hers. He was watching for an opening to jump her. Surely she'd been hurt in the blast; she'd just barely escaped death. As if to confirm his suspicions about her condition, Sonara's right knee buckled slightly when she moved to her right as Siren exited the lift car and walked to stand beside Nick. Siren glared daggers at her sister.

Nick watched Sonara's pale face become slick with perspiration and the hands gripping the rifle begin to tremble slightly.

151

Sonara cleared her throat. "I need to get to Feros III." Her voice trembled and the barrel of the rifle began to sag as if it had suddenly become too heavy.

"Why?" asked Siren haughtily.

"I..." The rifle slipped from her fingers and landed with a clatter on the deck. Then Sonara sagged as if she were a puppet whose strings had been cut. Nick watched in horror as she dropped to her knees, her head sagging forward, then finally collapsed facedown, her legs and arms askew.

Siren rushed to kneel next to her sister's side and pressed two fingers on the left side of her neck where one of the three carotid arteries were located. "She's alive. SIN, emergency transport. Two to the medical bay." Siren and her stricken sister disappeared in the sparkling glow of the materializer beam.

"Asia, meet me in the medical bay," Nick said into the comm unit in the wall.

Not waiting for his mentor's reply, he walked to the lift and, once inside, instructed the car to take him to the medical bay. When he arrived he found Siren, hovering over the control screen of a medical pod and peering at the screen reading the data about Sonara, her eyes flitting back and forth. The bay always had a slight chemical smell to him.

But he was never sure if it was real or a figment of his imagination about how all medical bays were supposed to smell. Of course, it could be a suppressed memory from the time he broke his leg when he was ten and fell out of a tree on the Estuian world of Polos. He had been taken to a local medical facility for treatment. The Estuian were a little backward when it came to modern medical techniques so the facility stank of all sorts of strong chemical odors— something he'd never forgotten.

"Well?" Nick said.

"She's dying," said Siren simply. "Radiation poisoning."

Nick crossed his arms over his chest and watched his second in command work. The lift doors opened and Asia Call appeared. Nick looked at the woman who had made him who he was today as if seeing her for the first time.

"What were you and Sonara up to?" Nick asked. Asia hesitated. "Tell me, Asia, I need to know what she was doing on Feros III. She's tricked us before, and this time I need answers if I'm going to save this world."

Asia's eyes read as conflicted and confusion. "I'm sorry, Nick, but I can't say anything. It's top secret."

Nick snorted as anger flared in his belly. "Top secret says who? The Alliance Council? This so-called Master?" He stepped up and grabbed Asia by both shoulders and squeezed as he shook her. "If you don't tell me who's supplying the Ferosians with dangerous weapons, they will die either by their own ignorance or when that Alliance Navy fleet returns to scour their world of all life."

Nick released her and stepped back, trembling from the sudden rush of anger threatening to consume him. He hated himself for manhandling the woman who had loved him when he needed it after his family died. The only good thing was he didn't have a blaster handy right now.

Asia lowered her head to her chest and began to sob. Now he wanted to wrap her in his arms and comfort her, but he resisted the urge. He needed to stay focused on the problem before him.

"Tell me," Nick said again, hoping his tone suggested menace.

"Okay, you're right, Nick. I'm sure you and Siren have already figured out Sonara works for me. She was my undercover agent, infiltrating the mercenaries working for the Master." She paused and lifted her chin. She wiped away the tears from under her eyes with the back of one hand.

"Sorry, I'm not usually this emotional, even with the pain medicine." She took in a shaky breath to steady herself. Puffing out her cheeks, she exhaled and then continued. "Her assignment was to create a war between two Ferosian factions and make the mercenaries think they'd succeeded. What they didn't realize was she was sabotaging the weapons so they didn't work properly. We hoped the Ferosians would think the so-called Tuple were tricking them and they'd attack the Master's base on the mountain."

"And they would have expected a group of aliens to show up disguised as Ferosians like happened before. Meaning us," Nick finished, shaking his head. He glared at Asia. "This could have gone bad in too many ways to count. Our plan was by far the better one."

"So where are the Tuple…I mean the *real* Tuple?"

She nodded. "We suspect the Master wiped them out and sent his operatives to pose as the Tuple. I'm sorry, Nick, I—"

"Sir." Interrupted Gears over the comm.

"Go ahead," Nick said.

"The Alliance fleet has returned. They'll be in orbit around Feros III in two hours."

"When will we be in orbit?"

"In just over one hour."

Nick frowned. He had a plan in mind, but no one was going to like it, him included.

21

City of Lothos
Feros III
4150.11.12 Galactic

"HOW LONG UNTIL the Alliance Navy fleet gets here?" Nick asked into the portable hand comm he'd affixed to the shoulder of his flight suit before transporting to the surface. He'd decided not to use the usual ear comm since the locals would think he was talking to himself. If he ever thought someone was talking to themselves, he wasn't likely to trust them either.

"Twenty-seven minutes, Captain," Gears said. The tech genius' high-pitched voice sounded stranger than usual over the portable comm.

Nick took in a deep breath as he looked up at the tall glass and steel tower that Gears and the Kid had determined was the government headquarters of one of the two factions vying for control of this world.

He let his breath out slowly, then walked toward the guard post at the entrance to the building.

The three guards standing there were large, heavily muscled Mallorans, their jade-green eyes watchful of the crowd of Ferosians walking along the sidewalk past the entrance to the building. Nick had taken a chance by not wearing a disguise but, fortunately, no one he passed seemed to take any notice of him. That was until a Cretak suddenly yelled loudly that an alien was among them and the crowded street between Nick and the guard post cleared as the locals scattered like roaches when the light is turned on. The smells of cooked meat, perfumes, and abandoned sweet drinks spilled on the sidewalk to form pools of liquid enveloped him, filling his nose and mouth.

The guards had drawn their projectile weapons and were moving cautiously toward him, three paces apart, their guns aimed at his chest. "Don't move, alien scum," said the guard in the middle of the three. The slight bump in the tummy above the waistline told him this was the birther.

Nick froze where he stood, his arms away from his sides, his hands open and facing down, and waited.

He'd fully expected to be shot on sight but was relieved when they didn't shoot first and ask the embarrassing questions later. Of course, maybe they were going to ask the embarrassing questions first, then shoot?

"Take me to your leaders," Nick said. His words in his ear sounded strange so he knew the translator was working.

The three guards exchanged uneasy looks, then one of them holstered its gun and moved toward him. When he was close enough, the guard grabbed his arm and twisted him around until he had his back to his captors. Nick felt a cold ring of metal being put around his right wrist, then it tightened, cutting into his flesh. Then the guard pulled Nick's left arm behind him and placed an identical metal ring around his left wrist. There was a sharp ratcheting sound and the steel rings tightened around his wrists. Nick winced from the pain. There was a chain between the two rings so Nick was unable to bring his arms back to his sides.

One of the other guards now holstered his weapon and with one guard on each side, their hands each holding an arm, they began to walk him up the steps leading to the building entrance. Nick heard the footsteps of the third guard a few paces behind.

He hadn't heard the familiar sound of the third guard holstering his weapon so he assumed it was now aimed at his back.

"No funny business," the guard to his left said sternly.

What is this Ferosian talking about? I'm not telling jokes. "Where are you taking me?" he asked as the twin smoked-glass doors leading into the building's lobby swung outward to admit them.

"To our leaders, of course," said the birther gripping his right arm.

"Oh," Nick said, surprised it had been so easy.

"They've been expecting you," added the guard grasping his left arm, guiding him roughly across the smooth gray stone floor of the lobby. The guards' boot steps echoed off the high ceiling of the massive lobby as they headed for a bank of what appeared to be lifts.

There were Ferosians gathered in small clusters scattered around the otherwise barren lobby, speaking in low whispers to each other, their eyes flitting to Nick, then away as if looking directly at him would result in them being contaminated.

Normally he'd think contamination coming from a look was silly but the Ferosians hadn't had much contact with alien species, so how were they to know what he was or wasn't capable of?

160

As Nick often said, judging others wasn't his job.

Nick entered a lift car accompanied by two of the three guards. The third guard had stayed in the lobby.

One of the two remaining guards pressed a square button with a number on a panel on one side of the car and it began to move upward. Nick had the sensation of motion under his feet and in the pit of his stomach. Lifts on starships had built-in gravity compensators so the rider didn't feel the motion. This was an odd sensation.

The lift car stopped and the doors slid open onto a large room decorated with potted plants and numbers of chairs lined up in rows facing a long, black-topped table with stainless steel legs at either end. Seated on the opposite side of the table facing the rows of chairs were three grim-faced Ferosians with their fingers interlocked, their elbows resting on the table. Since these three Ferosians were Rocha, Nick knew they were government officials. They had sun-browned complexions and almond-shaped eyes common to the Rocha. They were dressed in unadorned sleeveless soft gray open-necked shirts and long pants. Visible under the table were their dark brown boots that appeared to Nick to be made of materials similar to leather. Like most Ferosians, they were completely hairless.

Their milk-chocolate irises followed the guards as they led Nick to the first row of chairs facing the table and pressed him into one. The guards retreated to the back of the room by the wall, where they waited silently.

"Who are you?" asked the Ferosian seated between the other two.

Here's goes nothing. This had better work. "My name is Nick Justice. I am the leader of a group of mercenaries known as Blaster Squad. Most importantly, I am here to stop you from destroying yourselves or being destroyed by a fleet of starships that are headed for your world."

The three Ferosians' eyes widened and the one who'd spoken before leaned forward in the chair. "Why should we believe an alien?"

"Because I have a starship orbiting your planet right now that could have destroyed the advanced weapons the Tuple provided you from orbit." He paused to let his words sink in, then added, "The Tuple you've met are not who they say they are."

The Ferosian to the initial speaker's right scoffed. "How can we believe any of this, Notkol? An alien's word can't be trusted."

Nick arched an eyebrow. *So this is Notkol.* "Because the weapons they gave you didn't work?"

The one in the center, who Nick assumed was Notkol, frowned. "How do you know this?"

"I captured a spy who had infiltrated the Tuple and discovered the truth behind those weapons and about the plot to wipe out your people to assume control of your world."

The one seated to the left of Notkol spoke next. "So what is this truth?"

"A being known as the Master has been plotting to overthrow the galaxy and planned to destroy all life on your world to use it as a base to attack a nearby galactic trading route."

The Ferosian to Notkol's right sneered. "This is utter fantasy."

Notkol's thin lips formed a wry smile and his green eyes flared slightly. "Nick Justice, it seems my colleagues don't believe you. I, on the other hand, prefer to keep an open mind. We have known about the Tuple living in Cloud City for some time but have kept it secret so we didn't create a panic amongst the people. If what you say is true, then how will you prove it if you can't change the minds of us, never mind an entire civilization?"

"Will you release me and let me contact my ship? I can prove everything I'm saying."

Notkol and his comrades exchanged looks, then Notkol signaled for the guards to come forward and remove the restraints. After they were off, Nick activated the portable comm. "Siren, how long until the Alliance fleet arrives in orbit?"

"Five minutes until the lead vessel makes orbital insertion, Captain," Siren's voice echoed off the meeting room walls. Nick saw the skepticism in the Ferosians' eyes.

"Patch me through to the Alliance Navy admiral on the command battlewagon."

"Are you sure, sir?"

"Just do it." Nick smiled weakly at the Ferosians, who looked no more convinced than before.

Another deeper, huskier voice came over the comm unit. "This is Admiral Schipp of the Alliance Navy. Who is this?"

"Admiral Schipp, sir, this is Nick Justice of the GSS *Hunter,* requesting you stand down."

"Ah, yes, Justice. Blaster Squad, isn't it?" He snorted derisively. "Why should I listen to some mercenary?"

"Well, sir, I've made first contact with the Ferosians and discovered someone has been supplying them with advanced weapons in violation of the Galactic Accords.

And I have the person responsible in my custody on my ship."

There was a lengthy pause, then an unhappy sounding Admiral Schipp said, "Of course. Thank you, Justice, we will stand by to lend assistance as needed." The comm went silent.

Nick smiled to himself. Under galactic law, if during a first contact mission it was discovered someone had violated the accords not to interfere with a primitive race, the Alliance must rectify the damage done and work to bring that infected world into the Alliance. Nick had used a loophole in the law to save this world from the Master and his allies.

"Sir." It was Gears. "A vessel is leaving Cloud City headed into orbit. According to these readings, a dozen or more of the saurian mercenaries are aboard. It appears they're trying to escape."

"Thanks, Gears. Patch me through to the admiral again."

An unhappy sounding Admiral Schipp came back on the comm. Nick suggested the navy give chase and capture the escaping pirates, telling him they were allies of the spy aboard his ship. Within a few minutes, Gears confirmed the Alliance fleet of ten ships had left orbit to catch up with the mercenary's vessel. They weren't taking any chances.

Nick smiled at Notkol, who appeared none too pleased. "What was that all about?" asked the Ferosians' leader.

"I think I just saved you from doomsday," Nick said with a chuckle.

22

IT TOOK SOME explaining, but eventually Nick and Asia convinced the Ferosian leadership from both continents they were telling the truth. Mostly it took transporting them aboard the *Hunter* to see their own world from orbit. It didn't hurt that Bones gave them a demonstration of the ship's weapons' capabilities for them to fully comprehend the dangers they might have faced if the Master's plan had succeeded.

Sure, he had stretched the law a little by telling Admiral Schipp, when he returned after vaporizing the pirates, that Nick's actual mission was a first contact authorized by Chairman Whizzar. And which Asia backed him up on as the Chairman's emissary to this world; but it worked, and at the end of the day, that was all that mattered.

167

Nick knew Asia was still hiding information from him but he agreed, albeit reluctantly, to let her stay on Feros III to help them recover from the interference by the pirate mercenaries working for the Master. Especially after Sonara disappeared once again, and with her died any possible lead back to the Master.

According to Siren, her sister had injected herself with a drug that mimicked the effects of radiation poisoning. A blood scan taken after Sonara was transported to the medical bay, and after Siren finally had the time to check, confirmed they had been tricked. Once they were distracted saving the galaxy and Sonara had recovered from the drug's effects, she escaped. Nick didn't know how she escaped but suspected Asia's involvement.

Asia told him Sonara had infiltrated the Master's organization and knew who he was, but hadn't told her before she disappeared. All Asia knew for certain was the Master was a member of the Alliance Council, just as Nick also suspected. Though his mentor had deceived him in the course of this mission, he wasn't going to give up on her just yet. In truth, Nick suspected Sonara was working for the Master.

"Where're we going next?" Siren asked.

Siren had taken her sister's deception better than Nick had thought she would. She explained that, as far as she was concerned, her sister had gone bad, but Nick knew that, deep down, the family bonds between the sisters were still strong. Siren's stoic outer shell would crumble eventually. He only hoped he was there to pick up the pieces when the realization that her sister might be working against them sank in.

"I'm not sure yet," he said. "Let's head for Earth and take some time off." He swiveled his chair in order to look around the flight deck at the slumped shoulders and weary expressions on his friends' drawn faces. "Blaster Squad needs a holiday."

A chorus of "Aye, aye, Captain!" met this announcement, followed by gales of laughter.

Blaster Squad will return in their next thrilling adventure, *Rise of the Empire*.

About the Author

International selling author, Russ Crossley, writes science fiction and fantasy, and mystery/suspense as well as their various subgenres.

His latest science fiction satire set in the far future, Revenge of the Lushites, is a sequel to Attack of the Lushites released in 2011. The latest title in the series was released in the fall of 2013. Both titles are available in e-book and trade paperback.

He has sold several short stories that have appeared in anthologies from various publishers including; WMG Publishing, Pocket Books, 53rd Street Publishing, and St. Martins Press.

He is a member of SF Canada and is past president of the Greater Vancouver Chapter of Romance Writers of America. He is also an alumni of the Oregon Coast Professional Fiction Writers Master Class taught by award winning author/editors, Kristine Katherine Rusch and Dean Wesley Smith.

Feel free to contact him on Facebook, Twitter, or his website http//:www.russcrossley.com. He loves to hear from readers.

Other titles by Russ Crossley you may enjoy
Razor and Edge Mysteries
The Kidnapping of Billy Buttons
String of Pearls
Death by Clown
Beggin' For Murder
Ragged Ice
The Grand Central Mystery
A Strange Case of Undead Murder

Jazz Stiletto Mysteries
A Day Without Sunshine
Skullduggery
Instrument of justice (first published in Over My
Dead Body online mystery magazine)

The Amanda Dark paranormal mysteries
Hook Island
Grind Manor
Moonrise Diner
A Father's Daughter

The Trudy Wilson Mystery Novel Series
Bad Loyalty
Shear Murder
Buzzcut - coming soon

Blaster Squad
#1 Terror on the Moon
#2 Sea of Death
#3 Planet of Doom
#4 Raiders of Cloud City

#5 Rise of the Empire

Other Novels

Attack of the Lushites
Revenge of the Lushites
My Zombie Prince
Antique Virgin
The Fire In Their Hearts
with R.S. Meger (from Champagne Books)
Zomopolis
The Last Serial Killer

Short Stories
Countdown
Shoeless Moe
Round Up At The Burger Bar:
The Story of Trixie Pug, Parts 1, 2, 3, 4, 5, 6, 7, 8, 9
Five Minutes
Blossom Queen, Barbarian
The Secret
The Family Line
End of the Flies
Death by Magic
The Penguin Sleeps With The Fishes
Only The Worthy
Hero For A Day
End of Empire
Strange Bedfellows
Big Business
A Perfect Crime
The Wise Guy and The Pirates

In Search of the Perfect Cup
T.I.N. Men
The Legend of G and the Dragonettes
The Incredible Mr. Fix-It
Lock Stock and Barrel
Divided Loyalties
Cave of Wonders
A Family Empire
Until We Meet Again
Dragon Rising
Solitary Man
The Keel Mountain Conspiracy
Angel on My Shoulder
Heroes of Old
The Great Bicycle Race
Tikka's Big Day
"My Partner the Zombie" —
Hungry For Your Love Anthology
(St. Martin's Press)
Big Hairy Deal
One Red Shoe
A Bad Day in Lunden Texas
Bloody Betty, Queen of the Pirates
Mirror Image
Dangerous Waters
Cape Disappointment
Boomerang
The Watcher of Wayburn Street
The Apprentice
Drip!
A Beautiful Friendship and The Parrot of Doom
Robine's Diary

The Christmas Club
Loose Ends
Splatter Pattern
It Takes Two
Lexicon
Replacement Parts
Sidekicks
Lost Stories
Time and Space
Survivors
Neighborhood Watch
Unnatural Immortal
Rum Runner's Lounge
It's A Small Galaxy
A Shattered Man
Betrayed
Replacement Parts
Clubhouse Heroes
Sounds That Angels Make
Muggins Rules – originally published in Fiction River
Volume 12, Risk Takers

Anthologies
Tales of Urban Fantasy
Five Tales of Bizarre Detectives
Tales of Mystery and Suspense
Tales of Weird Fantasy
Tales of Twisted Crime
Tales of The Unexpected
Tales From Space
10 by Russ Crossley
Round Up At The Burger Bar: The Story of Trixie

Pug,
Parts 1- 5 The Beginning
Worlds of Science Fiction and Fantasy
More Tales of Mystery and Suspense
Justice Served
Love Stories
Ladies of the Jolly Roger with Rita Schulz
The Adventures of Razor and Edge:
Five Tales From The Quirky Detective Team
An Unexpected Journey
On Edge
Thrilling Adventures
Total War
Courageous

Non-Fiction
The Writers Tools - The Synopsis

Also available from 53rd Street Publishing
http://www.53rdstreetpublishing.com

In this second mission in the 43rd century after an encounter with pirates Nick Justice leads Blaster Squad on a hazardous mission in uncharted space to rescue kidnapped aliens.

They soon become trapped in a mysterious void filled with a sea of lifeless alien vessels orbiting an artificial star powered by the powerful energy field they've been trying to recover.

Join mercenaries Nick, Siren, Gears, Bones, and the Kid as they discover a monstrous plot to dominate the galaxy. In a race against time they fight to escape this sea of death and must make a shocking decision before it's too late.

Blast off to far future with Blaster Squad in this tale of high adventure and pulse pounding action to save the galaxy for all human and alien kind.

An undercover operation can go sideways faster than you might think.

The alien's eyes scanned the faces of the four mercenaries until they settled on Nick. "You not Ferosian," he said in a way that suggested fact, not a guess.

The large alien spread his legs wider apart and his large right hand moved to hover over the butt of his holstered projectile weapon. "I'm count three, then we draw." His brow wrinkled deeper. "I kill you." His eyes flitted briefly to the alien still lying facedown in the street. "For Jerl."

Nick's mouth dried and his heart beat faster as a rush of adrenaline coursed through his veins. He wondered if this alien was a faster draw than he was. He hadn't tried a quick draw for a number of years. The quick draw wasn't used much anymore except in entertainment stories.

Nick shifted his feet and dropped his arms to his sides, then lifted his right hand until it hovered over the butt of his gun, mimicking the Rocha Ferosian's stance.

"One." The alien began the countdown.

It appears I'm being challenged to a duel. I'm about to find out if I'm as fast I hope I am.